GRAY BARKER'S NEWSLETTER

ISSUE NO 12   JULY, 1980

Major Urges Global Pact
To Avoid Interstellar War

'A POTENTIAL THREAT TO US!'

I0611829

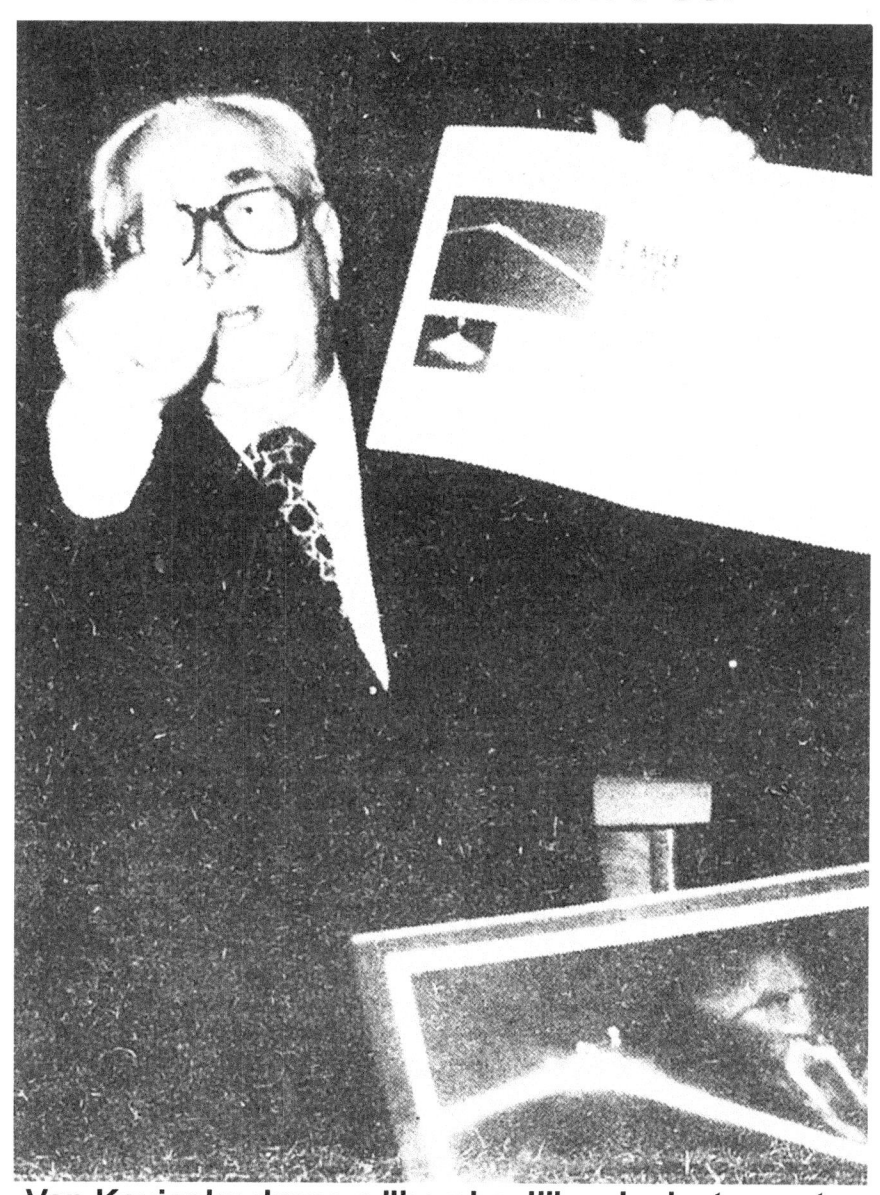

Von Kevicsky drops a "bombsell" as he lecturers to the House of Lords Select Commitee on UFOs

Gray Barker's Newsletter
No. 12 (July) 1980

Gray Baker
Alfred Steber (Editor)

SAUCERIAN PUBLISHER
Original Sources in Ufology

ISBN: 978-1-955087-59-9

9 781955 087599

INTRODUCTION

Gray Baker's Newsletter was a leading forum for personal experiences relating to UFOs, psychic abilities, ghosts and hauntings, cryptozoology, alternative medicine, and Fortean phenomena for a devoted readership worldwide. This title authentic reproduces the *Gray Baker's Newsletter* for July 1980. Grand but unpretentious, this issue is an extraordinarily rare symbol of what was going on in those early years of the modern UFO phenomena. Cover illustration of VonKevicsky addressing the House of Lords Select Committee on UFOs. Main topics in this issue: A conversation with VonKevicsky, the Philadelphia Experiment, the Iranian UFO Battle, the Dero and the Tero, the Mystery of Coral Castle, and many more.

This book has been formatted from its original newspaper size to a letter size for publication. IMPORTANT: although we have attempted to maintain the integrity of the issues accurately, the present reproduction could have minor defects and poor pictures due to the age of the original scanned copy.

Editor
Saucerian Publisher

Flying Saucer Investigator Gray Barker (May 2, 1925 – December 6, 1984)

Gray Barker's Documents

Gray Barker's Grave Site

Grayson R Barker
in the U.S., Find a Grave Index, 1600s-Current

Detail   Source

Name:	Grayson R Barker
Gender:	Male
Birth Date:	2 May 1925
Birth Place:	Braxton County, West Virginia, United States of America
Death Date:	6 Dec 1984
Death Place:	Braxton County, West Virginia, United States of America
Cemetery:	Barker Cemetery
Burial or Cremation Place:	Sutton, Braxton County, West Virginia, United States of America
Has Bio?:	Y
Father:	George Elliott Barker
Mother:	Rosa Lee Barker

Want to get involved? Click here.

ⓘ Report a problem

Photo added by R.C.

Grayson R "Gray" Barker

BIRTH	2 May 1925 Braxton County, West Virginia, USA
DEATH	6 Dec 1984 (aged 59) Braxton County, West Virginia, USA
BURIAL	Barker Cemetery Sutton, Braxton County, West Virginia, USA
MEMORIAL ID	181460934 · View Source

SHARE   ⊕ SAVE TO   SUGGEST EDITS ▾

MEMORIAL   PHOTOS ❹   FLOWERS ❸

Gray Roscoe Barker WWII Draft Card

FORM APPROVED
Budget Bureau No. 83-R012-42

REGISTRATION CARD (Men born on or after July 1, 1924, and on or before December 31, 1924)

(Also for the registration of men as they reach the 18th anniversary of the date of their birth on or after January 1, 1943.)

SERIAL NUMBER	1. NAME (Print)			ORDER NUMBER
W 159	Gray (First)	Roscoe (Middle)	Barker (Last)	11,688

2. PLACE OF RESIDENCE (Print)

Riffle		Braxton	W. Va.
(Number and street)	(Town, township, village, or city)	(County)	(State)

[THE PLACE OF RESIDENCE GIVEN ON LINE 2 ABOVE WILL DETERMINE LOCAL BOARD
JURISDICTION; LINE 2 OF REGISTRATION CERTIFICATE WILL BE IDENTICAL]

3. MAILING ADDRESS

Glenville, Gilmer Co., W. Va.

(Mailing address if other than place indicated on line 2. If same, insert word same)

4. TELEPHONE	5. AGE IN YEARS	6. PLACE OF BIRTH
	18	Riffle
		(Town or county)
	DATE OF BIRTH	
	May 2 1925	W. Va.
(Exchange) (Number)	(Mo.) (Day) (Yr.)	(State or country)

7. NAME AND ADDRESS OF PERSON WHO WILL ALWAYS KNOW YOUR ADDRESS

Mr. G. E. Barker, Riffle, W. Va. (father)

8. EMPLOYER'S NAME AND ADDRESS

None

9. PLACE OF EMPLOYMENT OR BUSINESS

(Number and street or R. F. D. number)	(Town)	(County)	(State)

I AFFIRM THAT I HAVE VERIFIED ABOVE ANSWERS AND THAT THEY ARE TRUE.

DSS Form 1 (Rev. 11-16-42)   a16—21630-4   (OVER)   *Gray Barker*

(Registrant's signature)

GRAY BARKER
P. O. BOX 2228
CLARKSBURG, W. VA.

January 30, 1960

J. Edgar Hoover, Dir.
Federal Bureau of Investigation
Washington 25, D.C.

Dear Mr. Hoover:

Leon Davidson, of 64 Prospect St., White Plains, N. Y., has sent me a copy
of a letter written to you under date of January 13th, expressing concern
over the outbreak of apparent Fascist activity, and suggesting some sort of
world-wide organization behind this movement.

Mr. Davidson, like myself, has written and published material about "Flying
Saucers," and the people he refers to are known generally as belonging to
the more or less "crackpot" fringe surrounding those who have tried to
investigate the subject seriously.

While I would not want to go as far as Mr. Davidson, in suggesting a sinister
organization behind or connected with these people, I do know that some of
the writings and literature connected with these fringe groups have contained
the "hate" line identified with the Nazis or Fascists.

I certainly hope that the amateur flying saucer investigating field, of which
I am a participant, does not become identified with the ideas of some of these
minority groups in our field.

While I really doubt that I could be of any real help to you, any of my files
certainly would be open to you in helping to cope with this situation of which
any citizen should be rightfully ashamed.

I might add that to my best knowledge, none of the saucer fringe groups are
tainted with anything which could be described as overtly following the Communist
line.

Very truly yours,

Gray Barker

REC- 35   157 - 3 - 6

EX - 131   FEB 19 1960

Not acknowledged due
to nature of letter - not worthy
due to fact Barker
has numerous 65 ref.

No ack
7/18/60

51 FEB 25 1960

Major Urges Global Pact To Avoid Interstellar War

'Stand Me Lord and be identified!'

The elderly guard in antiquated uniform dating from the days of the signing of the Magna Charta appeared too aged and weak to actually weild the huge war axe resting at his side, or to do much play with the sword in his scabbard. But he was a part of the ancient tradition still observed by the British houses of Parliament, and still a reminder of the grand day when freedom was wrested from the King of England.

The Hon. Brinsley le Poer Trench had with his a visitor which only he could have passed to the House of Lords chamber, and this happened to be some kind of ceremonial day, exactly what he didn't remember, when all of Parliament had to pretend that the Queen was trying to invade the legislature!

'Why I'm Clancarty, my good man. Ye know me well, and ye knew my father, as well as his father!

'A great man indeed, but who passes with you? Any man of the Queen's court must stand back and not enter!'

'No royalty indeed, the Earl of Clancarty replied, 'but a commoner and a foreigner, my good man, a visitor from the former Colonies, now America, who also distinguished himself in battle in Hungary and who fought with the Allies in the last war.'

'Ye may pass, me lord, as well as your companion. And a good day to you, General!'

The two men moved through a hallway lined with ancient armor. 'I'm sure you know your British history, Major, probably better than I, but I doubt if you are aware of some of the traditions, which sometimes get out of hand! All that fuss back there was over the tradition that the King or Queen cannot enter Parliament except on certain occasions, such as when they address the houses. I can't imagine why we have all that extraordinary security today. Who knows, maybe it's Guy Fawkes day!'

The tall, white-haired man with a military bearing grinned. Guy Fawkes had been a notorious anarchist who tried to blow up Parliament!

He liked the other man, and was just catching to his wry, underplayed sense of humor, such as his reference to the former Colonies.

Colman S. VonKeviczky walked with his sponsor, Trench (now Earl of Clancarty), onto the floor of the select House of Lords UFO Committee, where he had been invited to lecture on the existing global security and scientific problem created by more than three decades of UFO sightings. Clancarty had initiated the formal UFO Debate that recently had taken place in the House of Lords, and while there had been voiceferious opposition by skeptics, the body had ruled that a continuing study be set up, embodied by the formal Committee. Lords had invited not only VonKeviczky, but also spokesmen from England and European countries, to report on UFO research being done in the West.

Few would be equally qualified to speak for American research or possess the background of the Major. Born in Hungary, he was graduated from the historical Ludovica Military University in Budapest with a Master of Military Science and Engingeering degree. During 17 years of his distinguished military career, he completed more academic studies which qualified him for a promotion to major. Due to his skills in the field of com-munications, he was named Chief of the Audio-Visual Military Education Department of the Royal Hungarian General Staff and Ministry of Defense.

After 1945 he served seven years in an ex-change officers' program with the Third U.S. Army and Constabulary, and the International Refuge Organization in Europe. While in the program he contributed his skills as motion picture cameraman and director, and in public relations. He immigrated to the U.S. in 1952 and became an American citizen.

1

While a staff member of the United Nations Secretariat's Office of Public Information he became interested in the subject of UFOs after seeing secret documents and reading press coverage. Then after confidential talks with many diplomats and visiting scientists he became convinced that there was an unofficial 'cover-up' practiced by many governments which were puzzled by the phenomena and tended to try and 'sweep it under the carpet.' During a visit to France in 1963 he had an opportunity to confer unofficially with old military friends who had seen many startling official UFO reports and were deeply concerned about the problem.

But the skilled scientist woefully lacked expertise in another, even more specialized field - Washington politics - and this led to his undoing.

VonKeviczky made his fatal career mistake when in 1966, he submitted selections from his files of UFO evidence to Secretary General U. Thant, suggesting that the massive problem of UFO incursions be placed under international control, not only for exchanging information and developing a modus operandi for dealing with a potential threat, but for developing policies for communicating with the interplanetary visitors and legal philosophies that would be necessary, should the intruders land openly.

His arguments convinced U. Thant, who began holding delicate private talks with trusted diplomats. But the late Drew Pearson, predecessor of lack Anderson, sniffed out a leak and devoted a column to the Secretary General's interest in UFOs.

Readers may recall that these were the days after the convening of the Robertson Panel by the CIA and the decision to downplay UFOs in the public's mind. Powerful intelligence sources flushed out VonKeviczky as the source who had influenced the Secretary General and brought about pressures to dismiss him. Not only was he removed from the **U.N.** but he also was blacklisted as a scientist where Government employment was involved and became 'too hot to handle' in universities and the private sector where Government grant handouts often carried many informal 'conditions.'

VonKeviczky drops a bombshell as he lectures to the House of Lords Select Commitee on UFOs.

So like Baron Nicholas E. Von Poppen, whose secret of the crashed saucers was preserved by his fear of loss of political asylum (See Issue No. 11), VonKeviczky found it necessary to adapt to a lesser life style and to struggle for a living. Like Von Poppen, VonKeviczky turned to a technical skill for survival and became a commercial photographer. Eventually his growing clientele, along with a modest inheritance taken out of Hungary before the Communist takeover, enabled him to live comfortably and to set up his world non profit organization, the. Intercontinental **UFO** Research and Analytic Network, Inc. **(ICUFON)**.

The Major's "Bombshells'

'Highly Esteemed Chairman - Distinguished Peers of Her Majesty's House of Lords:" spoke VonKeviczky after the Committee Chairman Earl of Clancarty's introduction. 'I deem this my personal invitation requested by the noble Earl as an extreme privilege to enlighten you with our organization's 18 years of military, scientific and technological research, and to make you aware of the entire world's most acute and burning security and scientific problem.'

The major began his presentation with several 'bombshells' designed to surprise and shock his audience. One of his most startling revelations concerned the North American Air Defense Command **(NORAD)** in Colorado and its admission that sophisticated infrared sensors, satellite sentries and global network detect daily from 800 to 900 unidentified flying objects whose flight characteristics cannot be satellites or have ballistic trajectories.

"Now my Lords, these are alarming figures, even though one half might be discounted by your objective and skeptical minds. Even though, my noble audience, we reduce this to 304 Nay, not even this do I ask of you! Instead, gentlemen, let us accept only 104 of this figure and attribute it only to those objects which were **OBSERVED ONLY BY THE NAKED EYES OF WITNESS, OR FILMED WITH INEXPENSIVE CAMERAS, OR REPORTED ONLY IN THE NEWS MEDIA.**

'Even after discarding such massive scientific data, we are left with a frighenting summary:

'EVERY HOUR MORE THAN THREE OBJECTS OF EXTRATERRESTRIAL ORIGIN VIOLATE ILLEGALLY OUR GLOBAL AIRSPACES - TO KEEP UNDER CONTROL THE EARTHLY POWERS AND THEIR ACTIVITIES!'

VonKeviczky reviewed the massive missile buildup by the U.S. and the Soviet Union, despite pending **SALT** agreements, and then referred to a computer failure at **NORAD** during November, 1979, which could have touched off a nuclear war.

'The hazardous risk of continuing secrecy among nations on the subject of UFOs could at any time easily trigger a fatal misunderstanding, and activate between the superpowers the final holocaust of the third, and maybe even a space war.'

The Major suggested a solution. The military nations of the world should agree to immediately release from secrecy all of their UFO data that would not compromise their military systems and capabilities.

"This would not inflict the smallest damage to the official military secrecy of these nations."

Then he quoted Lord Kimberly who, speaking during the official UFO debate in Parliament on January 18, 1979: "**WE KNOW THAT WAR IN SPACE, ONCE A FIGMENT OF THE IMAGINATION, IS VERY NEARLY A FACT NOW.**'

A solution to the danger of an interplanetary war, as predicted by the late General Douglas MacArthur*, might be a beter understanding of the motives of the space invaders and mankind's reactions to them. In the U.S. these reactions had been largely hostile. He exposed armed actions against the UFOs, quoting Commanding General Benjamin Chidlaw of the U.S. Continental Air Defense that "the United States has lost many men and planes trying to intercept them."

VonKeviczky proposed a world organization to initiate a better understanding of the UFO problem. The first phase might be a voluntary alliance of the initiating nations for what might be termed a 'World Authority for Spatial Affairs," to be founded 'by the nations and for the nations' on a publicly donated ground territory. The resulting foundation should be governed by the associated nations and include representatives such as Military Forces, the Scientific Community, and even interested laymen who might represent the many private UFO research groups which had pioneered open studies and getting the information before the public.

The foundation's initial thrust would be in three fields:

(1) Combining the expertise of the best minds in each nation to secure expert analyses of UFO cases.

(2) Seeking ways to contact and communicate with UFO's in efforts to achieve mutual understanding and to avert hostilities on both sides.

3

(3) An educational program for the peoples of all nations to help them understand the problem of extraterrestrial intelligences.

VonKeviczky 'Scratched'

As VonKeviczky addressed the select gathering he was pleased and even surprised at the rapt and serious attention his presentation was receiving. And his mind flashed back to his troubles resulting from his efforts to secure in-terest in the United Nations toward goals he proposed.

Apparently, whatever persons or agencies were originally behind efforts to frustrate his efforts to gain international cooperation for UFO research were still very active in 1978. These new problems began after his receipt of a telegram from Sir Eric M. Gairy, Prime Minister of Grenada, who had employed his small nation's voice in the U.N. to promote UFO research. The telegram invited VonKeviczky to attend a meeting on July 13, 1978, with Kurt Waldheim, the Secretary General, and other parties. The meeting would discuss preliminary arrangements for Sir Gairy'a address to the General Assembly, scheduled for October of that year, and involve the development of documentary film presentations and exhibits on UFOs and related phenomena to complement the address.

But at the last minute VonKeviczky's part in the meeting was 'scratched,' on the excuse that scientists taking part did not approve of the Major's approach to the subject, and due to threats that they would not take part if he were present.**

"Japanese Saucers"

Much of VonKeviczky's presentation to the Committee is particularly interesting because it revealed much data heretofore never published, and no doubt obtained through his diplomatic and military connections. One such revelation is of a UFO "flap" predating the Kenneth Arnold sighting by five years:

On Feb. 25, 1942, 80 days after Pearl Harbor, a massive group of 15 to 20 DFOs carried out strategic reconnaisance along the U.S. Pacific costal territory between San Diego and San Francisco, perhaps to survey the huge concentration of manpower and military hardware staged there ready for embarkation to the Far East theatre.

"The whole area was alerted. According to the report of the 37th Anti Airborne Artillery Brigade, between 3:12 and 4:15 A.M., 1430 rounds of ammunition were fired in defense of Los Angeles at alleged "Japanese warplanes," though these "war-planes" were completely noiseless, and though a Los Angeles Times photograph unmistakably shows two wingless discshaped craft rounded by halos."

No bombs were dropped, and despite their relatively low speed of 100 miles per hour and altitude of less than 18,000 ft, no direct hits were apparently made.

"Chief of Staff Gen. George C. Marshall's secret report to President Roosevelt called the craft 'mysterious objects.'

'Of course the mysterious 'foo fighters' are better known. Sir Winston Churchill and General Dwight D. Eisenhower at first believed them to be Nazi secret weapons, until intelligence reports indicated the Germans thought just the opposite and that they were ours.'

In an apparent whack at his adversaries, Hynek and Vallee, VonKeviczky continued: 'We live in the reality of a three dimensional physical world, but according to certain 'scientific' theories we might exist within a multi-dimensional **INVISIBLE** world. But in reality, during the history of mankind, ghosts and spirits, though they have groaned and rattled their chains, have never created any real danger to humanity (laughter).

'This fundamental principle is self-evident in the U.S. General Staff's 30-year-old determination of the UFO evidence as consisting of 'nuts and bolts' - it is in the Summary Report on UFOs by Commanding general Nathaniel F. Twining, Chief of Staff of the U.S. Air Force, dated Sept. 18, 1947, submitted to his Chief of Staff, Gen. Omar N. Bradly. I think this statement should be considered a 'bit higher' than the private views of two astronomers)"

VonKeviczky quoted from Twining's report, recently (and perhaps accidentally declassified along with a volume of other material):

"(A) The phenomenon reported is something real and not visionary or fictitious.

"(B) They are objects probably approximating the shape of a disc, of such appreciable size as to appear to be as large as man-made aircraft.

'(C) Operating characteristics such as extreme rate of climb, maneuverability belief of the possibility that some of the objects are controlled either manually, automatically or remotely.

"(D) Apparent common description of the objects: (1) Metallic or light reflecting surface; (2) Absence of tail, except in a few instances when the objects apparently were operating under high performance conditions; (3) Circular or elliptical in shape, flat on bottom and domed on top; (4) Level flight speeds normally above 300 knots are estimated."

VonKeviczkv continued:

"To calm the concern of the public at large with UFOs, governmental sources prefer to accentuate that they are 'peaceful visitors' from outer space. The international UFO research community, too, widely advocates that UFOs are 'saviors' of our humanity.

A 'Political Problem'

"Let's examine this question with common sense and clear logic. How could we accept as **PEACEFUL INTENTION** any exploring extraterrestrial force, which over the decades has **NEGLECTED TO CONTACT AND COMMUNICATE WITH OUR NATIONAL OR INTERNATIONAL REPRESENTATIVES**, such as governments, the United Nations, NASA, scientists,etc? Should we formally accept that a superior space civilazation which has navigated for centuries around our celestial body should select for communication only socalled 'contactees' who are basically not qualified as well as educated to be a liason in any way. "

According to international law, aerial vehicles intruding illegally over nations' sovereign airspace affect their national securities. UFO forces, as 'illegal intruders,' should be affected. Thus the nations' armed action against them, **IN LACE OF INTERNATIONAL REGULATIONS WHICH I PROPOSED FOR THE U.N., ARE PERFECTLY LEGAL**. This aspect should be thoroughly studied by an international organization, lest an 'interplanetary war' be touched off.

I was impressed by a statement by Dr. Robert Spencer Carr, a noted expert in the field of non--verbal communications, who observed that, 'The problem of dealing with the UFO's is not a military problem primarily, but, instead, a **POLITICAL PROBLEM**."

As VonKeviczky's lengthy presentation drew to an end, he urged his audience to 'Lift the 30 years of military secrecy regarding UFOs. Voluntary nations should convoke a congress, represented by all the nations' military people, national academies of science, and UFO research groups, to determine, at long last, and before it is too late, **AGAINST WHAT HUMANITY IS FACING FROM OUTER SPACE!**

THE HOUR HAND ON THE PAGES OF MANKIND'S HISTORY IS VERY LATE. THE OPPORTUNITY TO RISE TO THE OCCASION AND ACT ON THE WORLD PEACE AND SECURITY OF THE NATIONS IS INDEED SUBLIMELY GREAT, AND IT MAY NEVER OCCUR AGAIN WITHIN OUR LIFETIMES".

On to Europe

Maj. Ret. Colman S. VonKeviczky arose at 9:00 A.M. on Sunday morning, a late hour luxury he permitted himself only on weekends and holidays. Not until late afternoon would he depart to France, the first stop on his European trip to gain acceptance of his ideas. He wondered about the effectiveness of his address to the House of Lords select Committee. True, reception to his remarks had been incredibly favorable, and members had kept him for hours afterward with their personal questions.

But so far the Press, though informed by his

official releases and personal interviews, had remained silent. Yet he was patient.

He had experienced all of this before. The downplaying of the UFO evidence may not have been the result of an official conspiracy as much as it had been an innate and 'natural one' - the inertia to resist radical new ideas and to preserve the status quo. Such as the refusal of the clergy to look through Galileo's telescope at the swirling rings of Saturn, or through Leeuwenhoek's microscope at the legions of paramecia which darted voluminously and relentessly as they fed and divided.

The Earl of Clancarty (left) meets privately with VonKeviczky. Clancarty (Brinsley is Poer Trench) is the author of several books about UFOs and related subjects.

But this was Sunday, and VonKeviczky vowed to take respite from his Mission and to relax, if even in his unfamiliar hotel room. He must not be so impatient!

Archimedes had boasted, 'Give me a lever and I can move the world!' And of course he had done it, but not literally. Instead he had moved an even greater weight, the minds of people from their hidebound inertial states. And he had not "moved the world' within his lifetime, nor had many other scientists who espoused radical and unpopular ideas. The General knew he too might not see his own ideas reach fruition.

He put on his dressing gown and ventured through the double windows onto the balcony outside his room for a few moments. Though it was late January, the temperature was surprisingly moderate for London. This city, this land, had witnessed the first birth of freedom, from serfdom and slavery, both of the body and the mind. Here the Magna Charta. Here the first effective legislature of the people. Here the Common Law, etched by an archetypal linotypist upon the soul of Western Man.

He hoped his House of Lords address had done some good, had planted some small kernel of truth, and that, like some Johnny Appleseed of his adopted country, his kernels would also grow.

But momentarily he forgot about all this, and his mission. Once again he imagined himself a child, bundled up, on a cold Sunday morning.

'Bless Father, Bless Mother, my Aunt Hildegarde in Dresden and Nurse Alexia.'

'What are you saying, Colman,' his waking wife asked from inside. He didn't answer immediately, being so captured—revery.

For the multitude of church bells, some near and voluble, but the most of them faraway; reminded VonKeviczky of his own little town of his birth, and of his native Hungary.

---

*General MacArthur stated on Oct. 5, 1955, that the nations of the Earth must someday make a common front against attack by people from other planets," and in June, 1962, at the West Point Military Academy, spoke of the "ultimate conflict between a united human race and the sinister forces of some planetary galaxy."

**Whoever "blackballed" VonKeviczky, the Major believed that Allen J. Hynek and Jacques Vallee were responsible. In a July 25, 1978, letter to Waldheim, he noted: 'To my great regret, my visit was suprisingly cancelled only a few hours before your meeting. It was excused by Sir Eric that our line of research does not meet the approval of the invited scientists' view on the UFO evidence."

VonKeviczky charged that Hynek/Vallee

"advocated the phenomena's reality on the basis of parapsychology, paranormal and 'beyond reality' theories, respresented by the respected scientists, Prof. J. Allen Hynek and Prof. Jacques Vallee."

Whether the General's inclusion in the meeting was "scratched' by the parties mentioned, or by the more "sinsisterm forces of the "coverup," cannot be pinned down. Our only genuine documentation is a copy of Sir Gairy's original telegram inviting VonKeviczky to attend. Our copy of the letter to Waldheim does point up the basic conflicts between VonKeviczky's 'nuts and bolts" approach to UFOs and the Hynek/Vallee "4-D" philosophy expressed in their writings, notably Vallee's **THE INVISIBLE COLLEGE** and their joint work, **THE EDGE OF REALITY: A PROGRESS RE-PORT ON UNIDENTIFIED FLYING OBJECTS.**

The full text of VonKeviczky's lecture before the Committee indicates he believes they may have been responsible for scuttling U.N. Interest:

"Ex-governmental and media promoted scientists are lecturing world wide about the UFOs' parapsychological existence, such as the pro-uncements of Drs. J. Allen Hynek, former USAF UFO consultant, and Jacques Vallee, whose pronouncments before the U.N. Special Political Committee on Nov. 17, 1978, that UFOs are 'beyond reality' and 'psycho-psychological phenom-ena' totally discredited the subject, which consequently was removed from the agenda, along with any further attention at the Committee on the Peaceful Uses of Outer Space.

VonKeviczky's mission to get U.N. sponsorship of his ideas was dealt a further blow when the government of Grenada was overthrown by a coup and Sir Gairy, the Major's chief ally in his efforts to get attention in that body, became an exile, and shorn of power after the most nations recognized the replacement government.

A Conversation With Maj Colman VonKeviczky

BARKER: Nell, Major, it certainly is nice to 'speak to you personally and get answers to some of the questions that came to mind as I was reviewing your House of Lords presentation. First I'd like to clarify your recommendations that the great military powers get together, share information, and work out common defenses for the threat of the UFOs. Would you elaborate on this?

VONKEVICZKY: Yes, the military authorities of all nations should cooperate. They could do this without giving away their own vital military secrets. They could agree to share **ONLY** that information relating to the UFOs which would not compromise purely military information. This cooperation might lead to further international efforts to prevent what I term an impending 'space war.'

BARKER: I assume this should also involve the scientific community?

VONKEVICZKY: Yes, the formal scientific establishment should be involved. But this should 'also include the participation and input of whom I term 'UFO pioneers, uch as yourself, representing the civilian interests, and at the same time contributing enormous amounts of data from the private sector.

BARKER: Do you believe that the UFOs represent a hostile threat to us, that they might be planning to attack us?

VONKEVICZKY: While I cannot, of course, read their minds, years of **ICUFON** research indicate that 80 percent of UFO surveillance involves military installations and quasi-military sites such as those where nuclear energy is researched and developed, or nuclear products manufactured. Much of this surveillance involves **SECRET** installations, indicating that the Galactic Force is well aware of our most highly secured operations.

BARKER: If a so-called 'intergalactic war'

should develop, and the UFOs attack us, would we have even a remote chance of defending ourselves against what may be a technology advanced many years ahead of ours?

VONKEVICZKY: Rather than address that question I would rather stress the idea of the peaceful establishment of contact and communication with these Galactic Enters, which is the only logical and common sense solution to the decades long deferring of the UFO problem. This is what I essentially stressed in my recent communication with President Reagan. I told him that the recent military secrecy and rash confrontation with the superior science and technology of the exploring space civilizations constitutes a rash act; no, I would rather call it an **INSANE** act. Speculating that we will gain by hostile action against them is, simply stated, an **IRRESPONSIBLE GAMBLE WITH THE EXISTENCE OF OUR CIVILIZATION**. Well, it seems I have addressed your question after all. But, again, let me stress **PEACEFUL** contacts rather than confrontation. Such contacts could bring immeasurable benefits for the Earth, such as **NEW ENERGY SOURCES**. Energy shortages pose threats from **WITH-IN**, which over the long haul may represent threats to our existence even greater than the speculated invasions from space. Communication would also stimulate a revival in science and technology throughout the world.

BARKER: Do you think it is possible to communicate with them?

VONKEVICZKY: Yes, this is possible, because the United States Military forces has very sophisticated technology that could accomplish this. While it is unlikely that such communication has not been carried out, I have no way of knowing because this subject is top secret.

Appeals to Reagan

BARKER: After your House of Lords presentation you went on to Europe to meet privately with UFO experts there. In England and France you complained that your news releases had been suppressed. Did these releases involve your Memorandum to President Reagan?

VONKEVICZKY: No, of course not. President Reagan was then not yet inaugurated. My remarks in Europe concerned my earlier releases. My Memorandum to Reagan was released on January 28, 1981 and first sought to redress my greviance of the Johnson Administration's placing me illegally on the notorious 'black list,' or security risk list of scientists. One of the important elements of this Memorandum was a review of my original proposals made to the United Nations in 1966 the business which originally got me - how do you say it? I have not yet a good command of the American slang idiom - perhaps it might be called 'on the hot seat'!

BARKER: Many of our readers are not familiar with those 1966 proposals. Could you boil these down for us briefly?

VONKEVICZKY: What?

BARKER: Could you summarize these proposals?

VONKEVICZKY: Oh yes. I was saying that the UFOs represent a potentially dangerous situation involving global security problems. I insisted that the UN was the logical agency to deal with this situation.

BARKER: How did you suggest that the UN go about accomplishing this?

VONKEVICZKY: **COMMUNICATION**. That was the key I stressed that might prevent a socalled 'space war.' I did not at that time suggest a military solution, but more of a political one. I said that the nations of our celestial-body should seek contact and communication with these extraterrestrial forces through an established International Authority. And what better authority than the UN, already in place? I backed up my recommendations with documentiation demonstrating that the galactic origin of these spacecraft had been confirmed by the military and space exploring superpowers, notably, of course, the US and USSR.

BARKER: Your ideas of stressing political solution remind me of statements made by Dr. Robert Spencer Carr. Do you know him?

VONKEVICZKY: No, but I do know of his work. He is a well known communications expert, who said, something like, 'The UFOs do not represent a military problem but purely a political problem.' While I do not go that far, I do respect his ideas, particularly his stressing communications, by way of a kind of 'cargo cult' methodology of building sheltered landing/communication sites. But I think he proposed a US unilateral approach, which I do not agree with. BARKER: Why not?

VONKEVICZKY: Because of the possibility of armed confrontation with the UFO forces, which is an **INTERNATIONAL** problem. Such a confrontation would not be with one nation regardless of what nation might provoke it. I have shown in my **BLUE MEMORANDUM** and in my House of Lords presentation that the US military and the military forces of other nations have attacked UFOs. Even if the superpowers might get together and agree to end such provocations, this would not prevent a small nation with an outmoded jet plane from firing upon UFOs and risking 'interplanetary war' over the whole globe:

BARKER: How can this be prevented?

VONKEVICZKY: The UN shows the most, and per-haps only promise, for dealing with this. Although it has not prevented all wars, it has worked remarkably well. Its charter provides for the establishment of fundamental international security. A potential war with the UFOs would threaten this international security. What I proposed was merely an extension of this doctrine which would involve the **UN** with an **OUTSIDE** intergalactic party or 'parties.

The Crashed Saucers

BARKER: What is your reaction to the rumors that UFOs have crashed and been captured?

VONKEVICZKY: So far the military has in its possession at least eight UFOs which originally were kept at Wright Patterson Air Force Base at Dayton, OH. Military scientists have studied these thoroughly, and that helped enable them to establish the communication technology I just spoke about. They have studied these since 1952, and now it is almost 1982 - that's 30 years, a long time.

BARKER: Have you, by. any chance, seen secret documents which have led you to make this state-ment?

VONKEVICZKY: Such documents admitting this have never been declassified. However, among the hundreds of documents that have been released, it is possible to put together a rather good scenario of the crashed discs and the analysis of them, and this process is basically the methodology **ICUFON** has employed. This is the basis for our statements in our **BLUE MEMORANDUM** which I have sent to you.

BARKER: Major, during your travels in Europe - in France, in Spain, Germany and so on, did you find that the authorities in these countries were any more open than this country in releasing UFO information to the public and admitting their ex-istence?

VONKEVICZKY: Gray, I have had talks with important people in many nations, even behind the Iron Curtain. In practically all these places, leading diplomats told me, 'The US and the USSR are the superpowers. They should take the lead, and once they do so, we will certainly fall in line and help to deal with this problem. But we cannot initiate it without the leadership and impetus they could provide. And of the two, we suspect the role of the US as an initiator could bring the other into it. Once this problem is given world wide exposure and definition, nobody, not even the USSR, can ignore it - and certainly not the leaser powers.'

BARKER: But the Soviets have consistently denied that UFOs exist and played down or sup-pressed sightings within Russia ...

VONKEVICZKY: This formerly was true. In 1966 when I originally presented my ideas to the UN, Soviet ambassador Trofimiirovich Fedoreno declared to the media that 'UFOs exist only in the night-mares of capitalistic imperialists headed by the US, and are used to stir up propaganda against the Socialist Republics.' Let me assure you, Gray, that this line is softening. Don't take my word for it alone. In more recent years Soviet Scientists have been given voice in the press to report on UFO sightings and to present all kinds of theories. And while I doubt that the Siberian explosion was the result of a UFO, as one of them insisted, such speculation did represent the softening of this official line. Remember that the Soviet press is controlled by and represents official government policy. Not only Russian scientists, but military authorities as well, have occasionally been quoted in regard to UFOs.

GRAY BARKER'S NEWSLETTER An official publications of the Space and Unexplained Celestial Events Research Society (SAUCERS). Published irregularly. Six issues $6.00. Exchanges with other UFO and related sines. Published by Saucerian Press. Inc., Box 2220, Clarksburg, WY 2001. Clippings and other UFO information needed.

Back issues Nos. .3 through 11 are available (See catalog inside or write for list.)

Hostility Against UFOs

BARKER: General, I know that you are recognized, particulary among your colleagues in the European **NATO** theatre, as a highly regarded military expert, but I must play the 'Devil's advocate' and remind you that you have been called 'irresponsible' by US officials in your insistence that our military forces are provoking hostilities by firing upon unidentified flying objects? Can you back up your claims?

VONKEVICZKY: Although I have hundreds of such cases in my files, I don't think you would have the patience to listen to them now, nor the space to print them. You or any responsible UFO re-searcher, however, are welcome to inspect these documents, upon prior arrangement, of course. I can summarize this for you however. To begin, perhaps you have seen the motion picture, '1941'?

BARKER: Yes, and it was a great disappointment to movie exhibitors, who hoped this Stephen Spielberg film would be as great as his **JAWS** and **CLOSE ENCOUNTERS OF THE THIRD KIND**

VONKEVICZKY: I agree that it was a disappointment, though as cinematographer I admired the special effects and the minature work. But it

was loosely based on an actual happening which took place, however, in the following year, 1942. In February of that year mysterious aircraft appeared over the West Coast. As you may recall, the Japanese had managed to direct some balloons carrying explosives to that area, and it was logical to assume that we were being attacked by enemy planes. Although the objects, when picked up by searchlights, appeared to be spherical or 'saucer' shaped, nobody had heard of 'flying saucers' at that time, and the mysterious foo fighters' had been assumed to be secret German weapons. So the military opened fire and shot more than 1400 rounds at the aerial armada. But they were either unable to hit anything (although the objects moved relatively slowly) or to bring any of them down. This understandable hysteria, incidentally, may have been one of the origins of later CIA fears that the UFOs might trigger a nuclear confrontration between the US and USSR because of misinterpretation. But that is a digression. The point I want to make is that the US began firing on UFOs in 1942 and has been firing on them ever since!

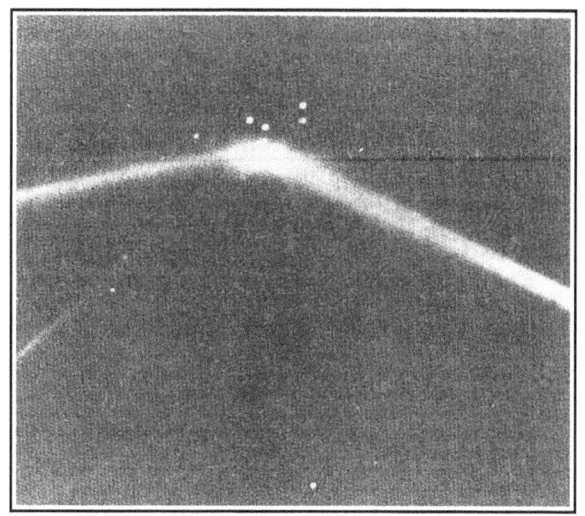

Searchlights pinpoint OR) over Ice Angeles the night of Feb. 24, 1942, and acic-ack guns fire at it. The military believed this (and other objects pictured) were Japanese planes. (Los Angeles TIMES photo).

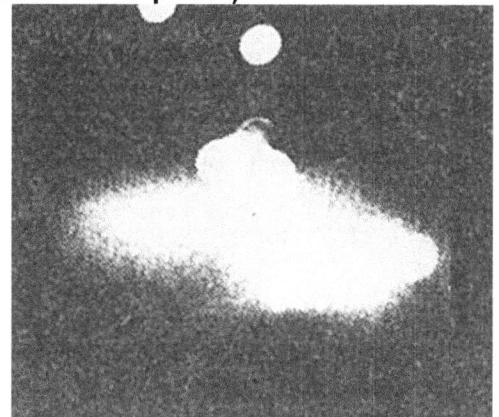

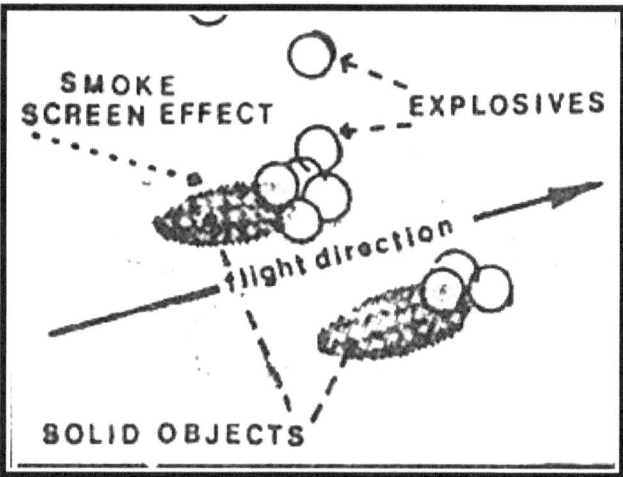

When searchlights are suppressed by darkroom technology discernible DISC-SHAPED objects are revealed (Drawing and enhancement courtesy ICUFON).

BARKER: Could the 1952 radar sightings over Washington, DC, when jets were scrambled to intercept what the military assumed to be enemy planes, represent a more modern analogy?

VONKEVICZKY: Of coursel I don't know if our interceptors were ordered to shoot at that time. That is still highly classified. By that date the authorities, though still insisting publicly that UPOs did not exist, had lost their naivete and may have been more cautious about confrontation. Immediately after these incidents (there were more than one of them), President Harry S. Truman asked Dr. Albert Einstein for suggestions. Though I, don't know why the President thought that Einstein knew anything about UFOs (though he held credit for initiating the development of nuclear weapons and may have been thought to know **EVERYTHING**), the mathematician did come up with a very sensible answer. "Do anything, but **DON'T SHOOT**," he told Truman. But Truman, whom I very much admire otherwise, shot from the leg (the General no doubt meant "shot from the hip" -GB). Six days later the Pentagon ordered jets to shoot down UFOs which refused to land when ordered.

BARKER: Did these attacks by our jets result in the crashed saucers you mentioned previously?

VONKEVICZKY: I don't think so. Some, if not all of these crashes, occurred before this general order went out. I don't know what happened in those cases. Carr (Dr. Robert Spencer Carr) believes that these UFOs were somehow disabled by our radar before they developed countermeasures, but to me this doesn't sound very logical, though I do not have technical expertise in that area. As best I can piece all this together, the UFOs generally eluded the intercepting and attacking jets, though in a few incidents our pilots were killed. The advanced technology of the objects is well illustrated by the recent incident in Iran which you may be familiar with.

BARKER: Yes, I'm printing a separate item about this in this issue. But to my knowledge these losses of our pilots have never been revealed, except for Capt. Mantell, now thought to have blacked out due to lack of oxygen at high altitude while chasing what probably was a Skyhook Balloon.

VONKEVICZKY, These incidents were highly classified for more than one reason. First there was the fear of panic, though this may have been an excuse for the general rule to classify most everything. Then there was the problem with the many organized civilian groups who were studying UFOs and in some cases even claiming to communicate with them, though I doubt that. These groups who believed the 'space people' were friendly and out to 'save us' might set up a hue and cry, and already there were rumblings in Congress due to Maj. Donald E. Keyhoe's demands for investigatiion of what he believed was a government 'coverup.' But the socalled "coverup' was not as tight as some have supposed. A careful review of recently released and declassified documents and even clippings from the press reveal that high officials even made public statements to the effect that the UFOs were real.

BARKER: Major, that is difficult to believe! Can you cite these instances?

VONKEVICZKY: I think I found some of these when preparing for your phone call. (Pause) Yes. Yes. Now I am quoting. First the late General George C. Marshall, Chief of Staff between 1947 and 1949. He declared, The United States Authorities have established the fact that flying saucers are manned by visitors from outer spate. Then there is the now generally forgotten statement by General Benjamin Chidlaw, head of the US Continental Air Defense, who said, 'We take them seriously when you consider we have lost many men and planes trying to intercept them. Even the US State Department had similar comments.

BARKER: Let's return to the subject of crashed UPOs. Now I know that there is so much rumor and circumstantial evidence that one cannot just dismiss all this. But there are many reasons to doubt these rumors. In my mind the chief reason Jar If a craft built by a superior civilization is examined by our scientists, why has this technology that they have surely learned not shown up in our society? Such an opportunity should give us a quantum leap ....

VONKEVICZKY: Some of it has shown up, mainly in our space program, and more of it will come out some day. Some of this knowledge may have military applications which we may have duplicated but hesitate to use for fear it might be copied by the USSR.

BARKER: Now, Coleman, I can agree partially with that, but there is a flaw in this. Many experts will tell you that the **REAL** threat to our globe arises not from the UFOs, but from energy starvation which may eventually overtake us and which has already thrown the world into near economic chaos. The UFOs must operate on a radical source of energy, and a very compact and cheap one, considering the vast distances they must travel. I just can't believe our government would withold this information, not only from our own citizens who are suffering debilitating inflation as a result of high energy prices, but because of the inate humanitarian concerns for the rest of the world that our nation has long demonstrated.

VONKEVICZKY, But that is the one thing they could not learn -the source of energy that powered these crashed discs. I understand that when, upon the one occasion of President Eisenhower's personal visits to one of the crash sites, he learned of this, he angrily cursed the scientists there and called them 'dummies.' But as I understand it they couldn't solve this mystery. In fact they couldn't discover **ANY** means of proplusion **WHATSOEVER!**

The Robertson Panel

BARKER, That is a fascinating area, but again, let's change the subject before our time and space runs out. In your **BLUE MEMORANDUM** you reproduce some documents about the Robertson Panel, sponsored by the CIA. One of these names Dr. Allen I Hynek as a panel participant, and I notice it gives him proper credit as a consultant to the Air Force Project Bluebook, whose policies he has largely renounced. But this document also names lynek as an 'OSI Consultant.' This sounds like an intelligence organization. Just what does the acronym, 'OSI,' stand for?

VONKEVICZKY: For the **Office of Scientific Intelligence**, which is a subsection of the CIA.

BARKER: But according to Dr. David M. Jacobs, whose book, **THE UFO CONTROVERSY IN AMERICA** (Indiana University Press 1975) is considered an authority on the Robertson Panel, Hynek was only invited to selected meetings, leaving the impression he provided only limited input, if any, to the proceedings.

VONKEVICZKY: An official document dated Jan. 27, 1953, and declassified in 1977, provides a different reading. It states that Hynek seat in on all the sessions after the first day,' however it states he did not sign the report as an official group member .

BARKER: But as I understand it, Hynek attended the sessions **PRIMARILY** representing Project Bluebook.

Conversation

VONKEVICZKY: However we must remember that Hynek had been retained as a member of **OSI** previously - **BEFORE** he became a consultant to Project Bluebook.

BARKER: I brought this subject up because I understand that Hynek was involved, along with a colleague, Dr. Jacques Vallee, in your efforts to persuade the United Nations to take action regarding UFOs. You sent me a copy of a telegram from Sir Eric M. Gairy, Prime Minister of Grenada, inviting you to attend a meeting on July 13, 1978, at the New York Hilton prior to presenting a program to the Secretary General Kurt Waldheim. You were to discuss documentary film and other audio visual presentations you would review with Waldheim prior to...presenting them to the UN body. Hynek and Vallee had also been invited, along with others, including journalist Lee Speigel and astronaut Gordon Cooper. But at this last minute, **YOU WERE EXCLUDED FROM THIS MEETING ....**

VONKEVICZKY: Would you like to know why?

BARKER: Yes I would. That's the question I've been leading up to!

VONKEVICZKY: Hynek and Vallee informed Gairy they did not believe in my theories and that they, themselves, weren't certain just what the UFOs were.

BARKER: You're saying that they refused to attend if you were present?

VONKEVICZKY: That is correct! Apparently Gairy believed that their scientific credentials, and in particular, Hynek favorable publicity in the news media, would greatly overshadow my importance in convincing UN members. Privately he even mentioned Hynek position as a blue ribbon panel member of the National Enquirer investigation (chuckles). So I was thrown out. Once again my carefully planned strategies to gain UFO recognition of the UFO problem came to naught.

BARKER: Weren't your ideas used and carried out?

VONKEVICZKY: I had a big fight with Gairy about this. I told him that the psychological ideas espoused by Bynek and Vallee would have no effect in the UN. Because to get any action from such a body you must prove that security is threatened. The charter of the UN provided that questions which dealt with global security had absolute priority and must be taken up and acted upon. My evidence proved just this, and this was the only line with which we could hope for a breakthrough. The UN would be unimpressed by 'other dimensions' or 'ghosts,' which Hynek and Vallee were talking about! But Gairy, who was very religious and himself bordering upon the mystic, became very greatly impressed with their parapsychological line. When he adopted it he became discredited in the UN, as I had predicted, and his ideas, which previously had been considered with some skepticism, now became untenable, and his efforts were completely ineffective.

BARKER: I have a question about Gairy, whose country, Grenada - by the way, where is it

13

located?

VONKEVICZKY: It's a very small island in the Carribean. BARKER: And Sir Gairy, he was not only its prime minister, but he represented his country, personally, in the United Nations?

VONKEVICZKY: That is correct.

BARKER: I understand that after this period we were reviewing, when you were working with him to get the UFO question before the UN, that there was a coup in his country, and his government fell, leaving him an exile.

VONKEVICZKY: Yee. I understand that he is no: living in California, but I have not communicated with him since the coup.

BARKER: Do you think the change in government in Grenada had anything to do with his interest in UFOs, or, because of this or some other reason, engineered by an outside intelligence agency?

VONKEVICZKY: No.

BARKER: Again, regarding Dr. Hynek. Do I understand you correctly? Are you saying he convinced a lot of people at the UN that the UFOs were not a threat to us?

VONKEVICZKY: Yea. During the Acapulco Congress in 1977 I screened the military documentation and I proved with genuine photographs that the General Twining report of 1917 to the Chief of Staff of the United States was completely true, because my photos showed that he was '1000 pecent' correct. After I screened these documents I confronted Dr. Hynek and and told him, 'You, Dr. Hynek, have twenty years of access to information while with the United States Air Force, but you say you don't know if they exist. Yet here is the military evidence that these UFOs are solid objects. Now what is your reaction to the evidence, Professor?' Do you know what he said? 'I'm sorry don't understand your question."I This exchange took place in front of the entire panel.

BARKER: I could have understood your position some years ago when he was a consultant for the Air Force and OSI, and participated in the Robertson Panel which probably had a major role in persuading the military to play down and ridicule UFO sightings. But this is 1981 and Hynek has reversed his thinking since leaving those positions. In fact he now heads the Center Por UFO Studies, a major civilian agency for disseminating UFO data. What about that?

VONKEVICZKY: Let me say that we have more than 4,000 documents on file, from many military sources, all contributing to our proof that UFOs do exist and are solid objects. Yet in **NONE** of these documents can I find his name. This might be explained by his being only an astronomical consultant. Perhaps this expertise with which you and others attempt to endow him was gained by some sort of 'crash course' after he left those positions.

BARKER: Our time is almost up and there are so many questions I no doubt have failed to ask you. Just one of my many remaining notes is about your petition to President Reagan. I have seen a copy of a letter you received from President Reagan before the election. Do you feel that the new administration will react more positively to the need for dealing more realisticaly with the UFO problem?

VONKEVICZKY: Gray, I am always optimistic, but I do not want to discuss this matter while my petition is under consideration by the President. But let me reiterate that I hold you in high esteem as a "UFO pioneer, and hope that I can call upon you for participation should there be a real breakthrough.

BARKER: Thank you, very much, Colman, for that compliment, and for your time and effort to grant this interview. My only regret is that, considering the enormous amount of information you have to impart, I may have only scratched the surface. I do hope I have helped you to present at least a general overview of your ideas to our readers. I hate to end this, but we must. I do wonder if you have any final thought, any short concluding statement that might help sum up your work?

VONKEVICZKY: That is difficult to do, but perhaps a statement from the US State Department's International Security Deputy Director, Michael A. G. Michaud, released in June, 1978, might suffice.

He stated: "**ALIENS PROM OUTER SOLAR SYSTEMS ARE A POTENTIAL THREAT TO US AND WE ARE A POTENTIAL THREAT TO THEM**".

BARKER: That's an excellent 'wrap up," Major! Good Night.

VONKEVICZKY: Good Night!

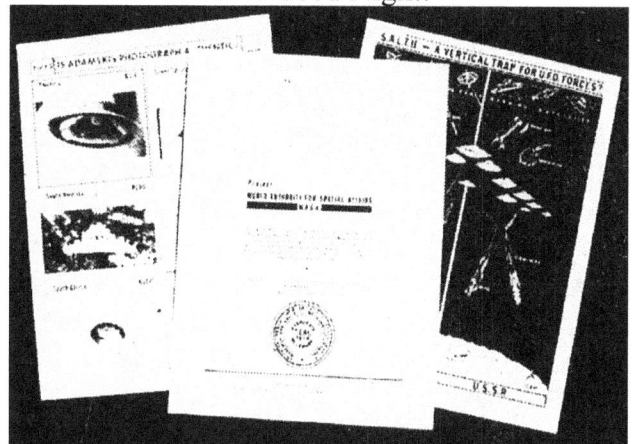

Please don't write to the NEWLETTER for copies of VonKeviczky's Memos. They most be ordered direct from ICUPON. The following publications are available: NASA Project (BLUE MEMORANDUM) - 110 pages Illustrated, $13.80 postpaid in US, Can. and Hex.; Other countries, $25.00 U.N. (GREEN MEMORANDUM) - 86 pages Illustrated, $13.80 postpaid in US, Can. and Mex. Other countries, $18.50 Address orders, checks or money orders to: ICUPON ARCHIVES Inc., 35-40 75th St., Suite No. 4G, Jackson Heights, NY 11372 U.S.

Return of The Philadelphia Experiment

Dear Mr. Barker:

I have hesitated to write to you, fearing you might take me for a crank. But I must no longer fear my own interest. As you can see from my purchase from your publishing company, I have a great deal of interest in the alleged Philadelphia Experiment.

For some time I have been interested in Einstein's Special and General Theories of Relativity and a new found interest in his Unified Field Theory, although references to this are hard to find. In fact I would like to state that I think the rejection of this theory because it was so seemingly incomprehensible is a scientific Cop Out. As far as relativity is concerned we know that the speed of light is unobtainable by material objects.

The belief that the mass of an object accelerating in space is absolute and unchangeable is in error. A ship of high velocity, let's say 90% of the speed of light, would greatly increase its mass due to the energy of motion ($E=MC^2$), If a ship approached the speed of light its mass would increase to near infinity. Since a body of infinite mass would offer infinite resistance to motion, this would prevent any such material object to attain the speed of light.

I am sure you are aware of the vast distances in space between ourselves and our neighboring stars, which are probably populated with advanced forms of extraterrestrial life. Now a ship of high acceleration would greatly slow its passage of time from its occupants' frame of reference and would decrease the distance between us and their ship at high speed. Yet it would still take a ship from, let's say, a star 4.5 light years away, four and a half years to reach us at the unobtainable speed of light. This refers to our frame of reference relative to the traveling ship. I know this may have been confusing so far, but please bear me out. It is unlikely that our space visitors have an origin in this solar system, although they may have established bases in it. These vast dis-tances, particularly of stars further out in the Milky Nay, or in other galaxies, and the attendant time frames in traversing these distances, have encouraged scientists such as Dr. Allen J. Hynek to question the extraterrestrial hypothesis.

But there may be an easy way out, and **THE PHILADELPHIA EXPERIMENT MAY PROVE THIS!**

In a book, **THE HAUNTED UNIVERSE**, (Signet 1977) by D. Scott Rogo, is a chapter titled, "Teleportation." Rogo, a prominent parapsychologist and UFO researcher, reveals a special briefing session held for the late Ivan Sanderson by Pentagon officials. During the briefing Sanderson casually asked if he could talk to any scientist experimenting with teleportation. According to Rogo, all Bell broke lose at that point in the briefing:

One official screamed, **WE DON'T MENTION THAT SUBJECT!**" Another said, 'ANYHOW, WE DON'T CALL IT 'TELEPORTATION' ANY MORE; WE CALL IT 'ITF'** (Instantaneous Transferrence)!' Let's stop and think about this for a moment. If Rogo is correct, this could mean that a space ship (or a Navy ship as the Pentagon officials may have been referring to) may not be restricted to the speed of light but might be transferred from one place to another **INSTANTANEOUSLY**, relatiye to all other frames of reference.

Einstein believed that Gravity and Magnetism were not mysterious forces but were simply the effects of the properties of space and time around them. He explained that objects did not exist in space, but were spatially extended. His Unified Field Theory sought to unite these aspects of the space and time continuum within one basic super-structure of universal law. When he proved energy and mass equivalences ($E=MC2$), he did not realise (until later, when he wrote to President Roosevelt) the destructive forces that could be derived from this in form of that atomic bomb.

Perhaps even Einstein himself was unaware of applications that might be made of his Unified Field Theory. And if he did, he might have re-tracted it, as Allende has suggested - for he was a great humanitarian and was disturbed by the use of scientific knowledge as a means of destruction. And perhaps this Theory holds potentials for danger even greater than that revealed by the Philadelphia Experiment.

If 'ITF' is possible, than our skies should be buzzing with curious extraterrestrial neighbors just passing through our neighborhood. And this just may be the easel Note that many researchers have stressed the role of gravity, its harnessing, manipipulation of, etc., in their theories of UFO propulsion. For instance, should they be able to create their own indenpendent gravitational fields, they could perform the "impossible" maneuvers described by witnesses without killing their pilots

with the enormous G-forces thus generated. But many of these same researchers, who may have been on the right track, **HAVE BEEN UNABLE TO EXPLAIN HOW THESE OBJECTS HAVE BEEN WITNESSED TO VANISH INTO 'THIN AIR.** Some of these, including Hynek, have retreated some ground from the extraterrestrial hypothesis to speculate that the UFOs might originate in a new dimension. **BUT WHY COULD THEY NOT HAVE BEEN SIMPLY TRANSPORTED FROM SOME OTHER LOCATION IN OUR OWN SPACE TIME CONTNU-UM? TO HELL WITH INVISILITY! IF THE DE-173 WAS TRANSPORTED FROM PHILADELPHIA TO NORFOLK**, as Allende and others insist, **THIS COULD SOLVE MOST OF OUR SPACE TRAVEL PROBLEMS!**

Recently I watched a TV documententary in the **IN SEARCH OF** Series about a man who had allegedly discovered secrets of levitation and built, all by himself, a construction called Coral Castle, using huge stones weighing many tons each. Nobody ever found out how he did this for he had no modern technology to help him - only his ropes and pulleys and his strange ideas and experiments in electromagnetism which were said to have been as incomprehensible as Einstein's Unified Field Theory has been too much for the scientific community. This hermit builder sometimes mentioned a 'sweet 16' to the few people he ever talked to about his methods, and they assumed this reference might have been to a Lolita-like acquaintance! It never occurred to them that the Unified Field Theory contained 16 equations: ten for Gravity, and six for Electromagnetism! And since Coral Castle is located near Miami, we might also be able to haul in the Bermuda Triangle to help explain it! At least, these are some added little pieces to be added to the mystery.

Sometimes I can't blame the government if it is conducting a coverup: The greatest threat to our national security probably is not by our cur-ious space visitors, **BUT BY OUR REACTION TO THEM!** To many of us they represent a prize grab, the occupants to be pickled in formaldehyde and their advanced technology appropriated for our own greedy gains. We obviously are not mature enough to handle the technology we already possess, and that is one reason why we may be beneath their dignities to contact us and remain only a pitiful curiosity to them. But continue we must in our quest for knowledge about what the Hell is going on!

Sincerely yours, Brian Parks, 19615 Mildred Ave., Torrance, CA 90503

Dear Brian: I think your letter makes a lot of sense. As to Coral Castle, now that is one whale of a story. Elsewhere we are printing a picture of the building, along with a report by James W. Moseleys on this subject. GB.

Dear Mr. Barker, My name is Douglas Earl Rushford. I have done a lot of reading on Dr. Jessup, which recalls an incident while I was in Philadelphia.

I got robbed and had to get something to eat. I ran into some guys and started talking to one of them. He said, 'Come on with me.'Well, after listening to about an hour of some guy telling us' that God loves you and all this, me and the three other guys got one slice of bread and a bowl of onion soup. I stayed there that night and me and this guy started talking about space ships, and he says, 'Shit, that ain't nothing,' and then he told me how, when he was in the Navy back in 1941, him and some guys took part in what's called thin air, and that's why he's a bum today. That after the Navy saw that it was doing things to the men they just discharged him as a mental case. My friend died in his sleep that night.

Mr. Barker, I would like you to tell me everything you know about this thin air and the documents that you have. I feel I should try in every way to bring this to the people. I think that man wants me to do that and he knew I would and now he can rest. I'll stay in touch and what I learn I'll forward it to you.

Forever yours, D. E. Rushford, Rt 1, Box 22, Capron, Va 23829.

Dear Mr. Barker,

I have done some additional research on Robert Oppenheimer. I was wrong in assuming that he was the mysterious Dr. Reno, as I reported in a letter which you published. He couldn't be Oppen-heimer, for Oppenheimer has been dead too long. However, his brother Frank may still fit the picture, since he also retired 'to the hills half a continent away' from Philadelphia. It seems that he retired to Colorado when he refused to testify at the hearings. I don't know if he would have been alive at the time Moore says that he interviewed 'Dr. Reno,' or if he is still alive, but I will find out.

Since both brothers were involved in the Manhattan Project, and both brothers frequently visited the Springdale area during the development of the atomic bomb, he would fit the picture as well, and perhaps even better since he was less well known than Robert. At any rate, I still believe they were both involved in some manner with this whole affair, since the coincidence of the Springdale effort on the Manhattan Project, the visits to western Pennsylvania by these men, and the letters from Allende coming from New Kensington are just too much for the odds. That combined with the other information I was able to get from Dad before his death has me convinced that these men were in some way connected with both projects. While Frank was a theoretical physicist as opposed to an experimental physicist, he was known to be a better experimental physicist than Robert in many ways. He had both the ability and the kind of mind that it would take to think of something like the Philadelphia Experiment. The more I research him, the more I am intrigued by his mind, and now am becoming more understanding of why my father was so enamoured of his abilities. Dad always said that he thought him to be superior in many ways (mentally) to almost any man alive at that time. I will keep you posted whenI find out any more.

Sincerely, Florence Michael

Ed. Note: It may be necessary to reread Michael's letters in Issues Nos. 10 and 11 to fully appreciate the above. While I have never presumed to ask William Moore if one of the Oppenheimers were indeed "Dr. Reno, he did volunteer, on one occasion, that Michael's letters had been "very interesting." -- GB

Mr. Barker and Mr. Moore.

I would like to contribute some info to you re: The Phila incident. I was assigned to the Eldrige from day of launch at Port Newark, NJ (7/43), and left it around 10/45. It was **THE ONLY SHIP** I was on during my Navy time - Now this may have happened in between sometimes as we were in Phila a few times during (undecipherable). Read enclosed history of the ship. Ships names are not duplicated in the USN.

Capt. Van Allen was on it from launch to decommission in Green Cove Springs, Fla in 45. He is an attorney in Charlotte, NC.

Moore G Van Allen Attys.

3000 NCNB Plaza

Charlotte, NC 28280

Phone 704-374-1300

So something is wrong - or not not known. Hope I helped in some small way.

(Unsigned)

Note: We have telephoned Capt. Van Allen, who acknowledged he was the commanding officer of the ship, but insisted **HE HAD NEVER BEEN IN PHILADELPHIA!** Recently we have been in touch with researchers (other than William Moore) who claim they have uncovered evidence indicating that the Eldridge **WAS NOT THE SHIP INVOLVED IN THE EXPERIMENT**, but that's all we can say about this right now--

Dear Mr. Barker,

While attending a Navy electronics school in 1976 I heard a very interesting but vague account of an experiment in which a Navy ship and its crew were said to have become invisible. We were studying magnetics at the time. The instructor said the experiment involved creating a strong magnetic field about the ship, but he knew little else about the project.

I dismissed this account as just another BS story told to pass the time on a slow day. It wasn't until about a month ago when a friend and I were discussing the possile use of levitation or antigravity to move the huge stones of Coral Castle in Florida that I again heard of this experiment. My friend turned me on to the book, **THE PHILADELPHIA EXPERIMENT**, by W. L. Moore. Very well researched and written.

Anyway I got your address from this book and understand I can obtain a facsiimile copy of the **VARO ANNOTATED EDITION** of Jessup's **THE CASE FOR THE UFO** from you. Can I still get a copy of this book or any other information on this subject? Any help will be appreciated by the both of us!

Sincerely,

Steve Cummings, 709 Oxford Dr., Virginia Veach, VA 23452. Dear Steve:

Am sending you some advertising literature on the VARO EDITION and related publications we handle. Your letter reminded me about the mystery of how Coral Castle was constructed, and I'll try to dig up some information on this and print it elsewhere in this issue. - GB

Dear Mr. Barker,

I have been interested in unexplained phenomena for a very long time. But what intrigues me most of all is the notorious Philadelphia Experiment.

I live in the vicinity of the Philadelphia Naval Base and the alleged occurrence has emerged as something of a local legend here, and is a topic of intense debate. I have inquired among many South Philadelphians about this enigma, and those who can recall it emphasize wholehertedly its validity. However, my parents, Basil and Edith Merenda, cannot recall it, even though my father was a naval veteran of WW II and both of my parents had business in the area around the Naval base at that time.

But they do remember the then existing taverns frequented by sailors, where the 'ruckus' described by Allende and the Moore/Berlitz book may have taken place. The favorite watering hole of the Philadelphia seamen was the Big House which is no longer in existence. It was located at Broad Street and Oregon Avenue.

Sincerely, Joseph J. Merenda.

Prof. Philip Ianna, Leander McCormick Observatory, Charlottesville, VA

Dear Dr. Ianna:

I am reliably informed that you recently held a meeting with Carlos M. Allende (alias Carl Allen) to discuss his rather controversial theories and beliefs.

As you no doubt know, Allende's material contributed largely to the current book, **THE PHILALDELPHIA EXPERIMENT**, coauthored by Charles Herlitz and William Moore. As a member of the more moderate wing of OPO belief, I am doing a study of the book and the material that went into it. I would therefore appreciate greatly your taking the time to explain to me briefly your apparent concurrence with the Allende approach. As a member of the academic community, your endorsement of his claims carries a great deal of weight.

Any help you can give our Society will be most appreciated.

Sincerely, James W. Moseley, P.O. Box 163, Port Lee, NJ 07024, Ph (201) 869-8053.

James N. Moseley, c/o **SAUCER CHEER** publication, PO box 163, Ft. Lee, NJ 07024

Dear Jim: I disagree with "D.L." and his theory that the famous Phiadelphia Experiment couldt not have taken place in World War II because the advanced technology did not exist at the time. The fact was that the incredible technology used to build the atomic bomb made the technology involved in the Philadelphia Experiment look like a minor exercise.

Although it seems fantastic to cross the "dimensional barrier" with 1943 technology, how much more fantastic was it to "split the atom" and release the unlimited energy of the stars in 1945? If "D.L." would have asked any scientist before World War II whether an atomic bomb could have been constructed which could have been dropped by one airplane and destroyed an entire city in a fraction of a second, I am sure that these scientists would have stated that the possibility was the same as the imminent Second Coming of Christ.

Only the science fiction writers, especially H. G. Wells, predicted the coming of atomic energy with any accuracy. Similarly, the development of jets, rockets and radar during the war would have seemed like the most incredible science fiction only a few years before 1939. Again, the technology used in building these devices was probably more advanced than the equipment involved in the Philadelphia Experiment.

I believe that the experiment with the invisible ship did take place and that it was a disaster to the men involved. The Government does not like to admit such mistakes, and that could be the reason why the official story has never been released.

As for the brains behind this experiment, I believe that Nikola Tesla devised the apparatus before he died - ten months before the experiment took place in October 1943. Tesla had more experience than anybody else in the world in the field of high energy physics, and his experiments in 1900 producing artificial lightning on a large scale has only been duplicated in recent years. It has been said that he was 100 years ahead of his time, and his inventions dealing with electricity definitely indicated he was thinking into the far future ....

It is possible that Tesla could have built the high energy apparatus used in the Philadelphia Experiment in a few weeks. Such a feat would have been merely a minor problem for him.

Sincerely, Michael Cohen

THE GOSPEL ACCORDING TO THE MEN IN BLACK

Dear Mr. Barker,

In view of what I mentioned in an earlier letter about apparitions, UFO's and government secrecy, I found your issue No. 11 particularly interesting. You mentioned a Dr. John C. Roberts, who, according to Dr. William C. Conway, had been railroaded into prison. Dr. Roberts had found a way of transmitting cosmic or free energy similar to that developed by Nicola Tesla. I have done some digging into the works of T. Henry Moray (who discovered Radiant Energy), and Wilhelm

Reich (discoverer of Orgone Energy), and into lesser known inventors' works.

In all cases their work, have been suppres-sed, some inventors having to pay with their lives because of their discoveries. Big industrial interests and government agencies have **DELIBERATELY** suppressed the development of this energy, available "from the air," for no other reason than to keep us under their control. This energy, if allowed to be developed, could give rise to a highly developed technology. UFO's make use of this free energy principle as well as the anti-gravity factor.

In addition to the above is the fact that this hidden hand of government works through sec-ret societies as an underground network, which have set themselves up to control all governments of this planet, **INCLUDING** church government. The Men In Black are merely an extension or arm of these secret groups, and these MIB are to suppress the truth wherever they find it, thus protecting the interests of their masters.

Now this brings us to the connection between UFO's and apparitions. The Blessed Mother has appeared many times since 1531 (Guadalope, Mexico), including here in Necedah, Wisconsin, warning us of this conspiracy. Saints and Angels have also appeared and given messages concerning these very things. Most of the past messages and apparitions have been suppressed by church authorities. As you know, those who have investigated UFOs and related phenomena have been harrased and threatened (some put out of business), told not to reveal what thet, know. Certain clergymen within the Catholic Church have tried to do the same to us. We have also had our share of trouble with the Men In Black. For example, they have tried to kndnap my mother on more than one occasion (once nearly succeeding in getting her into their car); they have shot at her and have told her through a locked doorway, "Go to your bishop in LaCrosse (Wisconsin) and tell him it is a hoax."

They have poisoned our farm animals and harassed us for years in an effort to get us to deny that the apparitions of the Blessed Virgin Mary ever took place. I have personally lived through this and I am determined to bring out the truth concerning this conspiracy. I have had my own encounter with a Man in Black or Sinister Strange' as I call them.

I hope this gives you a better idea of what I'm researching into. This will probably sound far fetched except to those who have done some serious work into the matter. I would appreciate anything *ore you may have on Dr. Roberts. Sincerely, Kenneth G. Van Hoof, Box 606, RR 2, Necedah, WI 54646

Dear Gray:

Many thanks for relaying the letter and information from Jerome Eden of the new "Planetary Professional Citizens Committee," which I have joined. He, like myself (and I believe you, too), definitely does not belong to the "sweetness and light" school re UFOs. I do not believe all the 'actions of the UFO aliens are bad for us - but certainly most of them seem to be. BUT - we take care of cattle, although were are in a sense ex-ploiting them. Our point of view, re your Men In Black theory and my belief in orbiting Skyislands and UFO satellites and inner-earth bases, mutilations and some mystrious murders, may yet prevail. One thing: Some of us have the courage of our convictions.

Of late I have experienced several more mysterious disappearances of material, which would seem absolutely incredible to the average person. Betty Hill has had the same sort of strange happenings. I don't know whether you have had such or not, but I do remember you couldn't find your copy of our original book contract in your files. Ray Palmer apparently experienced mysterious disappearances from the mails of shipments of his **FLYING SAUCERS** magazines - and I remember he warned Kenneth Arnold and Captain Smith against taking with them any samples of the materials that fell at Maury Island, but to mail them. Then the Air Force plane that WAS taking such samples crashed under very peculiar circumstances; **AND** the remains of what might have been a proplusive cylinder (like the Virginia "skystone" I had) disappeared.

With kind regards, Al (Commander Alvin E. Moore, author of **MYSTERY OF THE**

SKYMEN)

Dear Mr. Barker,

It appears that we also have some strange "happenings" in the U.K., according to a book I recently read called **THE UNINVITED.**

The strange affair occurred in a remote area, first with the appearance of a UFO, causing untold events, including the **DISAPPEARANCES** of a herd of cows and their **REAPPEARANCE** in another pasture some distance away! This happened on a number of occasions.

Another interesting point (I quote from the book): "Anyway, it wasn't that which frightened her, it was what the men in the car looked like. I say "man," but she swore to me that the men just didn't look normal, didn't look human. One of them apparently stayed in the car, the other one came to the door. She said the one at the door wore some sort of **DARK COLORED SUIT** and walked in a strange static way. It was his face that she says frightened her the most. The forehead was much larger than it should have been, the eyes were **REALLY PIERCING**, and the skin looked like it was made of wax."

My underlining -- does this not sound like **MIB**?

Yours Sincerely, Frank Rushworth, 'Chylan,' Penwartha, Coverack, Helston, Cornwall, England.

Dear Gray,

In reference to the letter about rock songs dealing with UFOs: not only is there a song about the Men In Black, but there is a "new wave" group here in the SF area called the **MIB**. One day when I was in downtown SF I came upon a newspaper stand with black spray painted graffiti on it. Along with the Chicano graffiti, it said, "Men In Black." I didn't know what to think of it at first, until much later I heard that a band by this name was appearing somewhere.

Also, the Jefferson Airplane (maybe in their Jefferson Starship persona) cut a little known disc called **HAVE YOU SEEN THE SAUCERS**?. Also, Neil Young, a predominantly country-folk type singer, did a song about the silver spaceships coming after the Big One drops, and picking up 'mother nature's silver seed' to take it to another "place in the sun." Evidently the UFO topic has really crept into popular lore .... and song!

Would it be OK with you if I published the **DERO AND THE TERO** poem in **SHAVERTRON**?

Yours, Richard Toronto, **SHAVERTRON**, 309 Coghlan St., Vallejo, Ca 94590

Dear Rich:

Permission hereby granted to reprint the poem. I am mentioning how to subscribe to your **SHAVERTRON** publication elsewhere in this issue. GB

Dear Gray;

In response to a letter in Issue No 11 by Christopheer Dietler about the Blue Oyster Cult and their Men In Black song, both you and the writer were puzzled by the reference to "**BALTHA-ZAR**," which you said you could not find in an occult encyclopedia. No wonder, because "Baltha-zar" is the name of one of the **THREE** Wise Men who visited the baby Jesus in the manger. The two other wise men were named !Caspar and Melchior.

Also, in response to the letter from Florence Michael (Marlene Harvey) concerning Messrs A, B and Jemi of the Varo edition of the book, **THE CASE FOR THE UFO**, she misunderstood the explanation of **TWINS** and Jemi for Gemini. It does **NOT** mean that two of the men were considered biological siblings but merely that two of the men, and possibly all three men, were from the constellation "Gemini' star group. Each man could have been from a different star **OR** planet within that constellation, and would refer to each other as "my twin" or "my brother." They Would naturally feel as brothers coming from the same planet or star and working on a strange planet, and the "twin" reference was merely to let anyone who caught on to their coded talk realize where they were from originally.

Cosmic Blessings! (Name witheld)

Dear....

I hope your comments stir up Florence Michael into writing some more interesting letters. As to Balthazar, five other readers have also pointed out the origin of this name. As a person brought up by near fundamentalist Methodist parents and who learned to recite all the books of the Bible and won contests in Sunday school, I should be embarrassed and am. Let me assure you and the other correspondents that I am doing twenty push-ups a day (which is a lot for mel) until this goof of memory is somehow expiated! GB

Dear Gray,

I don't know if you've heard of an album by the British punk group, The Stranglers," which got into the top 20 album charts with **THE GOSPEL ACCORDING TO THE MEN IN BLACK!** Apparently it drew on very familiar themes.

Best regards, Geoff Gilbertson, Trinity Cottage, 5, St. Andrew's St., Wells, Somerset. England.

PUBLISHER'S EDITORIAL

THE GREAT IRANIAN UFO BATTLE

While on the surface VonKevicsky's warnings of intergalactic war may sound like something out of a science fiction movie, his contentions that there have been hostile acts directed at UFOs by the military of different nations have been supported by the reporting of many such incidents throughout "flying saucer. history. True, some of these incidents have been officially denied and others may have been inaccurately reported throug' reasons of misinterpretation, or have represented only rumors. Since preparing the article about th Major and interviewing him, we have checked some of his sources and found them remarkably accurate.

One of his claims concerned an alleged incident over Iran during which potentially hostile acts were narrowly avoided. I listened to his reference to the incident without comment, for I had, in this instance, an excellent opportunity t, check this allegation.

For only a short time previously I had come into possession of an official government document which described the incident in full detail!

SSG Clifford E. Stone had obtained it under provisions of the Freedom of Information Act from the Department of Defense, on appeal, after his initial request was denied. The report made science fiction seem tame by comparison, and tended to back up the many other accounts and rumors reaching UFO researchers, even though they had been denied and 'explained," chiefly by the U.S. Air Force.

The covering letter accompanying the report stated:

'Records available within the Office of the Secretary of Defense (OSD) and Organization of the Joint Chiefs of Staff (OJCS) relating to the September 1976 UFO incident near Tehran, Iran, consist of one three-page message. A copy of this message is enclosed with three minor deletions deemed necessary to protect a confidential source.'

The Report follows:

CONFIDENTIAL IRAN REPORTED UFO SIGHTING TEHRAN, IRAN: 20 SEPT 76 FRANK B MCKENZIE, COL. USAF.

THIS REPORT FORWARDS INFORMATION CONCERNING THE SIGHTING OF AN UFO IN IRAN ON 19 SEPTEMBER 1976.

A. AT ABOUT 1230 AM ON 19 SEPTEMBER 1976 THE (Deletion) RECEIVED FOUR TELEPHONE CALLS FROM CITIZENS LIVING IN THE SHEMIRAN AREA OF TEHRAN SAYING THAT THEY HAD SEEN STRANGE OBJECTS IN THE SKY. SOME REPORTED A KIND OF BIRD-LIKE OBJECT WHILE OTHERS REPORTED A HELICOPTER WITH A LIGET ON. THERE WERE NO HELICOPTERS AIRBORNE AT THAT TIME.

AFTER HE TOLD THE CITIZENS IT WAS ONLY STARS AND HAD TALKED TO MEHRABAD TOWER HE DECIDED TO LOOK FOR HIMSELF. HE NOTICED AN OBJECT IN THE SKY SIMILAR TO A STAR BIGGER AND BRIGHTER. HE DECIDED TO SCRAMBLE AN P-4 FROM SHAHROKHI APB TO INVESTIGATE.

B. AT 0130 HRS ON THE 19TH THE F-4

TOOK OFF AND PROCEEDED TO A POINT ABOUT 40 NM (nautical miles - GB) NORTH OF TEHRAN. DUE TO ITS BRILLIANCE THE OBJECT WAS EASILY VISIBLE FROM 70 MILES AWAY. AS THE F-4 APPROACHED A RANGE OF 25 NM HE LOST ALL INSTRUMENTATIONS AND COMMUNICATIONS (UHF AND INTERCOM). HE BROKE OFF THE INTERCEPT AND HEADED BACK TO SHAHROKHI. WHEN THE F-4 TURNED AWAY FROM THE OBJECT AND APPARENTLY WAS NO LONGER A THREAT TO IT THE AIRCRAFT REGAINED ALL INSTRUMENTATION AND COMMUNICATIONS. AT 0140 HRS A SECOND F-4 WAS LAUNCHED. THE BACKSFATER ACQUIRED A RADAR LOCK ON AT 17 NM, 12 O'CLOCK HIGH POSITION WITH THE VC (RATE OF CLOSURE AT 150 NMP). AS THE RANGE DECREASED TO 25 NM THE OBJECT MOVED AWAY AT A SPEED THAT WAS VISIBLE ON THE RADAR SCOPE AND STAYED AT 25 NM.

C. THE SIZE OF THE RADAR RETURN WAS COMPARABLE TO THAT OF A 707 TANKER. THE VISUAL SIZE OF THE OBJECT WAS DIFFICULT TO DISCERN BECAUSE OF ITS INTENSE BRILLIANCE. THE LIGHT THAT IT GAVE OFF WAS THAT OF FLASHING STROBE LIGHTS ARRANGED IN A RECTANGULAR PATTERN AND ALTERNATING BLUE, GREEN, RED AND ORANGE IN COLOR. THE SEQUENCE OF THE LIGHTS WAS SO FAST THAT ALL THE COLORS COULD BE SEEN AT ONCE. THE OBJECT AND THE PURSUING F-4 CONTINUED ON A COURSE TO THE SOUTH OF TEHRAN WHEN ANOTHER BRIGHTLY LIGHTED OBJECT, ESTIMATED TO BE ONE HALF TO ONE THIRD THE APPARENT SIZE OF THE NOON, CAME OUT OF THE ORIGINAL OBJECT. THIS SECOND OBJECT HEADED STRAIGHT TOWARD THE F-4 AT A VERY FAST RATE OF SPEED.

THE PILOT ATTEMPTED TO FIRE AN AIM-9 MISSILE AT THE OBJECT BUT AT THAT INSTANT HIS WEAPONS CONTROL PANEL WENT OFF AND HE LOST ALL COMMUNICATIONS (UHF AND INTERPHONE). AT THIS POINT THE PILOT INITIATED A TURN AND NEGATIVE G DIVE TO GET AWAY. AS HE TURNED THE OBJECT FELL IN TRAIL AT WHAT APPEARED TO BE ABOUT 3-4 NM. AS HE CONTINUED IN HIS TURN AWAY FROM THE PRIMARY OBJECT THE SEC-OND OBJECT WENT TO THE INSIDE OF HIS TURN THEN RETURNED TO THE PRIMARY OBJECT FOR A PERFECT RF JOIN.

D. SHORTLY AFTER THE SECOND OBJECT JOINED UP WITH THE PRIMARY OBJECT ANOTHER OBJECT APPEARED TO COME OUT OF THE OTHER SIDE OF THE PRIMARY OBJECT GOING STRAIGHT DOWN AT A GREAT RATE OF SPEED. THE F-4 CREW HAD REGAINED COMMUNICATIONS AND THE WEAPONS CONTROL PANEL AND WATCHED THE OBJECT AP-PROACH THE GROUND ANTICIPATING A LARGE EXPLOSION. THIS OBJECT APPEARED TO COME TO REST GENTLY ON THE EARTH AND CAST A VERY BRIGHT LIGHT OVER AN AREA OF ABOUT 2-3 KILOMETERS. THE CREW DESCENDED FROM THEIR ALTITUDE OF 25M TO 15M AND CONTINUED TO OBSERVE AND MARK THE OBJECT'S POSITION. THEY HAD SOME DIFFICULTY IN ADJUSTING THEIR NIGHT VISIBIL-ITY FOR LANDING SO AFTER ORBITING MEHRABAD A FEW TIMES THEY WENT OUT FOR A STRAIGHT IN LANDING. THERE WAS A LOT OF INTERFERENCE ON THE UHF AND EACH TIME THEY PASSED THROUGH A MAG. BEARING OF 150 DEGREE FROM MEHRABAD THEY LOST THEIR COMMUNICATIONS (UHF AND INTERPHONE) AND THE INS FLUCTUATED FROM 30 DEGREES - 50

DEGREES. THE ONE CIVIL AIRLINER THAT WAS APPROACHING MEHRABAD DURING THIS SAME TIME EXPERIENCED COMMUNICATIONS FAILURE IN THE SAME VICINITY (location undecipherable) BUT DID NOT REPORT SEEING ANYTHING. WHILE THE F-4 WAS ON A LONG FINAL APPROACH THE CREW NOTICED ANOTHER CYLINDER SHAPED OBJECT (ABOUT THE SIZE OF A T-BIRD AT 10M) WITH BRIGHT STEADY LIGHTS ON EACH END AND A FLASHER IN THE MIDDLE. WHEN QUERIED THE TOWER STATED THERE WAS NO OTHER KNOWN TRAFFIC IN THE AREA. DURING THE TIME THAT THE OBJECT PASSED OVER THE F-4 THE TOWER DID NOT HAVE A VISUAL ON IT BUT PICKED IT OP AFTER THE PILOT TOLD THEM TO LOOK BETWEEN THE MOUNTAINS AND THE REFINERY.

E. DURING DAYLIGHT THE F-4 CREW WAS TAKEN OUT TO THE AREA IN A HELICOPTER WHERE THE OBJECT AP-PARENTLY HAD LANDED. NOTHING WAS NOTICED AT THE SPOT WHERE THEY THOUGHT THE OBJECT LANDED (A DRY LAKE BED) BUT AS THEY CIRCLED OFF TO THE WEST OF THE AREA THEY PICKED UP A VERY NOTICEABLE BEEPER SIGNAL. AT THE POINT WHERE THE RETURN WAS THE LOUDEST WAS A SMALL HOUSE WITH A GARDEN. THEY LANDED AND ASKED THE PEOPLE WITHIN IF THEY HAD NOTICED ANYTHING STRANGE LAST NIGHT. THE PEOPLE TALKED ABOUT A LOUD NOISE AND A VERY BRIGHT LIGHT LIKE LIGHTENING. THE AIRCRAFT AND AREA WHERE THE OBJECT IS BELIEVED TO HAVE LANDED ARE BEING CHECKED FOR POSSIBLE RADIATION.

MORE INFORMATION WILL BE FORWARDED WHEN IT BECOMES AVAILABLE. PRIORITY

To our knowledge, this is the 'best' account of a UFO incident ever released officially by the US military, and its release may be due to its involving the Iranian Air Force and not our own. And it certainly is a 'textbook' incident, for it involves a number of 'classic" elements so long a part of UFO tradition, such as the failure of instruments, evasive maneuvers, brilliant strobe lighting, and even a mock attack by the UFO. Mysterious beeping radio signals at the landing site, reports of ground witnesses of a loud noise and brilliant lights, the release and retrieval of satellite objects from 'mother' craft - how many times have we heard these elements repeated in other sightings!

Although VonKeviczky seemed, in our interview, to be somewhat evasive when asked to comment on the question of hostile intent by UFOs, this may have been due to his wanting to stress peaceful communications with the aliens. And with very few exceptions, reports of military interceptions usually include evasive action by the saucers, with an occasional pretended hostile-like counterattack, called off at the last second with the veering off of the attacker.

The Tehran case in particular illustrates, however, the deadly potential the UFOs must have, should their occupants decide to engage in serious battle. A technology or telepathic mind that can render a firing mechanism inoperative at the very moment a terrestrial pilot decides to fire represents an adversary of so forminable a nature it would be almost inconcievable to hope to defend our world from them should they decide to invade!

VonKeviczky no doubt is aware of this, and this in probably why he is streesing communication. While he warnings of 'intergalactic war' may be stretching it bit, considering that our earth is still intact after more than 30 years of the modern 'flying saucer' era, this hyperbole may be for the benefit of the UN, which is more seriously impressed by threats of hostility than by le tangible ideas such as communication.

And the Iranian incident stresses his belief that neither the US nor any other nation should act unilaterily in deciding not to fire on UFOs or to try seriously to communicate with them. Without international control, countries such as Iran could easily upset the intergalactic applecart by continuing such hostilities. And should the UFOs be receptive to communication (and we don't even know if they are), common sense suggests that Earth won't be able to get very far in this direction until we call a "cease fire").

VonKeviczky has also stressed his "nuts and bolts" approach to Ufology and opposition to those theorists who believe the saucers may be interdimensional, metaphysical, or utterly incomprehensible to the human mind. Although they may have been able to inject themselves in a form understandable to their Iranian adversaries, their methods of battle illustrated by the above incident were quite human and terrestrial-like (though they exhibited a **MORAL** nature above mankind's in that they were able to conduct the mock battle without loss of life or without injury to the Iranians).

It is VonKeviczky's contention that others in the group taking part in the presentation to the United Nations scuttled the attempt to obtain international cooperation in dealing with the UFO problem, since their non-material, "4-D" ideas were not persuasive to the politically oriented membership, which could better understand a 'nuts and bolt" threat of 'intergalactic war.'

It is unfortunate and unconsciable that certain other parties refused to participate in the presentation unless VonKeviczky were "black-balled" and excluded. Due to his exclusion, the UN and the world may have been deprived of critical insights into a mystery that eventually the world must come to grips with, understand, and cooperate in order to deal with it intelligently. VonKeviczky, a European, saw the ravages of World War II from a first hand vantage point most Americans, particularly the present maturing generation, can never envisage nor sympathize with. Like Baron Nicholas E. Von Poppen, VonKeviczky saw his own country ravished, then come under the heel of Soviet dictatorial rule. Though one might never realize it from his accent and lack of familiarity with the American vocal idiom, in his acts and research can one read the fierce patriotism he accords to his new-found homeland, America. His war experiences, the loss of freedom by his former homeland, and other traumatic experiences may indeed color his frenetic drive to get his message across, and cause lesser men to doubt his motives.

Another Major, Donald E. Keyhoe, identified and railed against the Air Force coverup of UFOs, and was labeled "paranoic" by some of lesser vision. But Keyhoe's vision is now being proven by the release of military documents. It is ironic that such documents indicate that one of the very same men responsible for some of the Air Force "explanations" to counter Keyhoe's hell raising, was also one of those men responsible for excluding VonKeviczky from the UN presentation.

VonKeviczky, like Billy Mitchell, and even Keyhoe, may be one of those visionaries whose very strong partisanship to his cause may lead to misunderstanding of his ideas by others within the time frame of his heyday. His World War II experiences mentioned above could explain this partisanship: he does not want to see his new found home, nor his world community devastated and dominated by an intergalactic threat, however nebulous that idea may seem to those who do not have knowledge of his immense documentation of UFO incidents.

We have long wanted the opportunity to speak about those persons, whose reputations in Ufology hang precariously upon media attention and the prestige of their doctoral degrees rather than "dirt farmer" accomplishments in a field somewhat removed from their valid academic specialties; those whose poverty of practicality lead them to into esoteric wastelands where they may wander and pontificate without accountability; those who depend upon their publicity in the **National ENQUIRER** rather than engage in genuine **National INQUIRY**. In their exclusion of VonKeviczky from the UN discussion they have shown, perhaps, their fears and doubts of their own self-images. But why fear that VonKeviczky's presentation might overshadow their own? After all, had they not said privately in their derision that he was "incomprehensible"?

--------------- Gray Barker

25

THE DERO AND THE TERO

=================================

Palmer on "Shaver Mystery"

February 4, 1957
Dear Long John Nebel, NOR, NY:

Unfortunately I do not hear you here in Wisconsin, but your listeners give me a pretty comprehensive report regarding the portions of your program devoted to "The Shaver Mystery" and particularly to the remarks of Mr. Harlan Ellison, who has quoted me directly. For he record, I'd like to set that matter straight for you and your listeners.

Mr. Ellison tells of his question put to me in an elevator during the Chicago Science Fiction Convention, 'What about the Shaver Mystery?" He quotes my reply, "It was a publicity grabber to obtain circulation."

Here are the facts: The science fiction fans (that small group officially known as "tendon') had condemned the Shaver Mystery and me, the first as untrue, and myself as a "traitor to science fiction. Harlan Ellison was one of the prime movers in this condemnation. His group had needled me for years, and had resorted to open sneers at the convention. Naturally I was nettled. Nobody had asked me what was true about the Shaver Mystery; only how I could dare to pass off such a fake as a true story. Most of them, I discovered by a few questions, didn't even know what the Mystery was about, and in fact, some had not even read it! Thus, when cornered in the elevator (and this seemed to me to be a planned effort), Mr. Ellison, who put his question as a challenge, and not as a question, with the preconceived attitude that if I said it was true, I was a liar, and if I were honest, I'd say it was untrue, struck me as the least qualified to put such a question, as he was just a boy of about 17. I replied: "I'll give you the answer you want! It was a publicity stunt to increase circulation.

Long John, it was exactly that! It was dressed up in my best publicity getting style, and it increased circulation by 50,000 copies per month. But in the process of the dressing up, and of getting circulation, the **BASIC FACTS** in Mr. Shav-er's original story were retained **INTACT. I DID NOT** say that the Shaver Mystery was a hoax. I said it was a publicity and circulation getter, and a very effective one. Mr. Ellison has given my answer the connotation he desired all along. But it is his connotation. When I told other science fiction fans the story was true, they argued that it could not be. I would like to pass on my own opinion to you, and through you, to your listeners.

I accept the original Shaver manuscript, which he titled "A Warning to Future Man" (and which I retitled "I Remember Lemuria"), as the statement of a man who sincerely believes every word he has said is the truth. As an editor,I expanded the basic 10,000 word manuscript to 31,000 words, and added the 'action' and "plot flavor" that would make it read less like a dull recitation. I did not change the names of the characters; I introduced no new ones; I did not change the "history' of events as outlined in the original manuscript. I merely dramatized them, added dialogue, of which there was none in the original, and which we, as publishers of a magazine of entertaining stories, absolutely demanded a manuscript to have.

I have investigated the so called Shaver Mystery for fourteen years, and have come to the very definite conclusion that Mr. Shaver spoke precisely the truth to me, as he saw it. I have gone much further than Mr. Shaver in my efforts to corroborate his story, and I believe that I have amassed a tremendous file of supporting evidence. I am firmly convinced that the things Mr. Shaver says happened to him, did happen to him, and that his report is true and logical in his deductions, and that the part rationalization plays in it is also logical and extremely shrewd.

During my investigations, I have had certain experiences of my own. These experiences are available to anyone interested. In the case of prejudiced investigators such as Harlan Ellison, it seems futile to repeat them. I will give you an example:

I went to Pennsylvania to visit Mr. Shaver, and while there, heard his "voices of cavern people. If I repeat that to Mr. Ellison and his group, they make this flat statement: 'You have just given us evidence of paranoic symptoms." Or, they say: 'Shaver must have wired the house, and deceived you.' Or, "You have been the victim of your own imagination.To such a biased investigator I suggest that the questioning be eliminat-ed, and to save time (mine) simply make their own flat statements. Mr. Ellison has not heard the voices, and I humbly suggest that he is indeed fortunate! Mr. Ellison has never encountered a "dero," and I positively say, he is fortunate beyond all belief.

Thus, will you report to your listeners that, to those who refuse to accept a Positive answer, I freely give the negative one: 'I ran the Shaver story as a circulation getter, and it was very successful." To those who are willing to consider that I have a right to give anything but a prescribed answer, I say: 'The Shaver Mystery has been factually reported, and to the best of my knowledge, based on many years of research, is true; and further, that I have my own opinions, which differ in some minor facets from the opinions of Mr. Shaver himself."

As an example, Mr. Shaver refers to the caves without puting the word 'cave" in quotes. He hears the voices, he looks up, they are not there, he looks around, they are not there, ergo, they can only be underground. He eliminates **UP**, because some of the voices mention specific distances (I myself heard them refer to 'four miles away and four miles **DOWN**), and because, including the equipment they say they have, they would be perfectly visible if they were in the air at that distance.

I put the word "cave" in quotes, because two other possibilities suggest themselves to me, which also have scientific evidence to lend them credence, and thus I cannot be positive which is the actual location. One possibility is the newest (and seriously propounded) scientific theory that another dimensional existence is possible, and in fact, does exist, popularly termed 'the fourth dimension"; the other possibilty (and this seems also to possess a fourth dimensional quality) is that the caves are "astral," or associated with what those who believe in life after death as the location to which departed spirits go.

I deduce it extremely possible that **ALL THREE** possibilities may be involved here; ie. there **ARE** actual caves, with living people; there **ARE** other dimensions, with living people; there **ARE** spirit worlds, with what we call 'dead' people.

I have sent men into actual caves. Some reported "nothing." Others reported 'strange psychic experiences.' One reported 'a smooth bore, slanting steeply downward, obviously artificial,' and in spite of my request that he leave it alone, or investigate it with sufficient help to insure against accident, he went back with ropes, mountain climbing equipment, oxygen mask, and was never heard from again. Also, he refused to give the location of the bore. It may be that he anticipated great treasure (certainly the machines Shaver mentions would be tremendously valuable!), and didn't want his "claim' to be usurped by others.

Mr. Shaver performed, and I actually participated in, certain specific actions which cannot be explained unless his story is basically sound and true.

1. He predicted the flying saucers, literally and accurately, two years before they were seen.

2. He named the day of Nikola Tesla's death, in a letter to me.

3. He described hundreds of scientific advances which I have watched become facts through the years. Not just generalizations, which any science fiction writer can do, but mathematically exact representations.

There is a vast file of such things. I can't mention them here. But just as the nature of matter is a mystery, yet matter is a fact; the nature of electricity is a mystery, yet electricity is a fact; the nature of the universe is a mystery, yet the universe is a fact - so the nature of the Shaver Mystery is a mystery, yet it is a fact!

I have a suggestion to make to Mr. Harlan Ellison. If he will, in the privacy of his own bedroom, make a violent commotion, fling his shoes upon the floor, and in a loud voice, demand that the dero prove their existence to him in a way that will make it impossible for him to prove it to anyone else (such as burning him to death in his bed without burning the bed clothes, or having a car run him down at a specific location undisclosed to anyone but himself), I feel that it is quite possible that they will oblige him. At the same time, I suggest that he refrain with all his might from doing so, because I can tell him personally that I'm quite sure that it is possible he will get results, and I would not like him to come to harm. For, if he were to face me in an elevator and make such a demand in my presence, I would dislike being in the elevator with him. In short, it would be the better part of valor to remain outside with the angels, and not join the fools in their rush to get inside.

Incidentally, I am sending this letter to you via my friend, Gray Barker, who has appeared on your program, and possibly will again. In the event that he does, I appoint him as my official representative, and if you desire further information,I shall endeavor to provide him with this, for his appearance. If you desire any specific information from me, I shall be happy to answer any letters you care to write me.

Sincerely yours, Ray Palmer, Rt 2, Box 36, Amherst, Wisc.

Note: Later, probably in the mid-60's, Palmer had an opportunity to appear, along with Shaver, on the Long John Show, via telephone. Through a lot of luck, we were able to obtain a high quality recording of that one-hour segment, and have made it available in cassette tape form, at $7.95. If you wish to order this, add $1.00 for postage and handling and write to us in care of **THE NEWSLETTER** (Or use order blank from our catalog). - GB

Spacemen Among Us?

Dear Mr. Barker:

If I ever met the man of MY dreams on a UFO, I'd not blink an eye! Of course I have no proof that this wasn't an ordinary earth man. I have only my own years of experience and knowledge. And of all places to see such a guy!

At the outside window line of Bank of America, I was bored to death. Maybe that's why I began to observe this man closely. He was about 6' l, and suddenly he swung around and looked me squarely in the eye. Maybe he picked up my thoughts. He asked if I wanted to try for weight. (Of course I had opened the conversation. I'm a great talker. I love humanity and only want to be of service.) I missed on weight. I guessed 145 lbs, but this guy said he weighed 185. Ha hal! I figured he must be full of "heavy water.' He was so slim but had such a fine body. Dressed well. Short jacket like some service use - some sort of silvery-white stuff. Tight trousers but good. Good shoes. It was his overall beauty that got me. The essence of masculinity without the animal look some earthlings have. Gorgeous brown eyes. Pearly teeth. I sound like-a pulp writer but I can see that man yeti Black hair, well cut except for about two inches too long in back - straight across.

He was clean shaven and had a beautiful voice. Enchanting smile. I said to him, 'If you didn't have that cigarette in your hand, you could easily pass for a UFO occupant.' With that, he tossed the unlighted cigarette away, looked me in the eye and said, '**NOW** do you believe?'

Mr. Barker, he looked so happy. I thought it so odd when he remarked about the beauty of the trees in the Plaza opposite because there were nothing but bare branches except for a very few old time cedars, fir or what have you. Thought I, where in the devil did **YOU** come from! This was early spring of this year. Then he did such a sweet thing: All this outside ground is the same level and cars swish right and left. It's a miracle that nobody's been hit, but I wasn't paying any attention whatsoever. This guy puts out a long arm around me like a horseshoe. He didn't touch me - just protected me until any danger was past. He was the last word in being gentlemanly. I listened when he reached the window. He said something about not having his pass book. Then, of all things, he drove off in a yellow Dodge pickup! I've never seen this beautiful man again. But the plot thickens:

Some time afterward, this Modesto contactee phones my friend and says he has a message for me. The message:

Tell Emma I'll be in the Bay Area soon and we'll get together!

Well, Mr. Barker, very shortly after that, comes this UFO over the hills here, a very spectacular sighting, but I've never laid eyes on my man again. I wouldn't exactly call this 'getting together,' but as Robert Burns said: the best laid plans o mice and men gae aft aglee.

My best thoughts to you, Miss Emma P. Martinelli, 681 First St. West, 46, Sonoma, CA 95476.

Dear Mr. Barker,

As I study further into occultism and mysticism, strange ideas and conclusions come to mind. All occult study stresses the practice of regular, daily meditation, of the clearing of the mind from physical sensation, and leaving it in a state to receive, by some means or another, meaningful intuitive knowledge from a higher source. Occult study slowly works at awakening and developing the chakras, the energy vortexes within the human body, especially the pituitary and pineal glands, which, as I think I mentioned before, act as transformers, among other things, lowering the vibrational rates of extrasensory phenomena to a rate that can be perceived by us.

The teachings are of the highest and finest ideals. They always teach, above all, our obligations of service to mankind, of helping our fellow human beings in their evolution of unselfishness and kindness and love. And of leaving our minds receptive, during meditation, to intuitive guidance from beyond.

What strange things come to mind as I study more and more into the UFO field. Are the entities from beyond who guide us the same as the higher type entities associated with the UFOs? Are we being prepared to receive communication with these entities, our forefathers, perhaps, who wish to guide us and help us evolve further? I've read, especially in Jacques Vallee's books, where religious miracles were tied in with UFO encounters, and UFO encounters compared to mystical experiences, and even the final great experience of Cosmic Consciousness. Perhaps they all come from the same source, I just don't know. I can't draw any conclusions with what limited experience and knowledge I have. But my curiosity couldn't be greater!

Are the UFO entities the same as the angels of ancient writings? Are the fairies and elves of medieval folklore the same as the lower elemental beings of occultism, and are both the same as the lower sort of entities reported in UFO literature? I hope that before I die I find out some answers to these questions. I would hate to go through transition from this life totally ignorant of any of the answers to these questions, and have to wait until next time around to pick up where I left off.

Mr. Barker, best wishes to you, and may all the **MIS** that cross your path be friendly!

Sincerely, Carolyn C. Coven, 4822 Luann Ave.. Toledo, OH 46323

Dear Mr. Barker:

As you know, I an erecting what will be the largest privately-owned telescope in the U.S.

I am also conducting investigations of UFO cases and assure any witness of complete confidentiality. Although I work closely with you, I will refer these invetigation results to you only with the express permission of witnesses.

Very truly yours, Richard P. Taylor, 104 Highland St., Gassaway, WV 26624. Phone (304) 364-2477. Dear Richard:

Am happy you have decided to offer your consultation services. I have known you for several years and can vouch for your expertise and integrity. In fact, I urge readers to first report their data to you for evaluation and investigation, after which they can be referred to me for further analysis and possible publication. -- Gray.

"Yes, my Doctor is sending me to the Sea of Clouds for a change of vacuum."

IN & OUT ZINES:

----Black Holes and White Bumps----

'Since UFOs display unearthly performance characteristics and apparently come from outer space, it is reasonable to assume that their propulsion systems are somehow connected with outer space,' believes Kenneth W. Behrendt in an article titled, 'UFO Propulsion Systems', Origins, and Purposes.'

And what phenomena in outer space would be as portable to stow on board a saucer and as powerful a gravitational influence as - you guessed it, **BLACK HOLES**! But such baggage might be hazardous to the crew, considering their abilities to suck everything into them. Yet Behrendt gets around this one neatly by proposing the **OPPOSITES** of Black Holes, which he accepts as **WHITE BUMPS**; and which **REPEL**

matter with the same intensity that the Black Holes attract it. Bring along a couple of these which are a bit out of balance and you could nullify the frightening properties of each, with some energy left over, to the extent the duo was unbalanced.

Behrendt has not just one, but two imaginative articles on UFO propulsion theories, in **THE SIXTH QUARK** JOURNAL (Published by Tom Benson, P.O. Box 1174, Trenton, NJ 08606 - 6 ishes $10.00, or $2.50 per ish), an 8 1/2 x 11', 56 pager. Although some of the material is rather technical, the average lay UFO enthusiasts should be able to understand most of it, and it is excellently illustrated with diagrams and other drawings. On the lighter side, the zine includes a sexual encounter case and a book review. Issue reviewed is No. 1, so we don't know how the 'SIXTH° part of the title is derived. Have there been other Quark Journals published previously, maybe on other dimensional planes? After reading this excellent effort, I suggest that explanation!

To Witches at Saucerian Press

Book customers on the Saucerian Press mailing list prefer books about Contactee Stories, Lost Continents, Men In Black and the Hollow Earth, in that order, according to a study made by David Stupple and Abdollah Dashti (Eastern Michigan Univ and Univ of Michigan). A questionnaire forwarded to a sampling of such customers also firmly established that they had no use for witches or Satanists - for only 18 and 12 per cent of the nearly 400 people responding indicated interest in books about those subjects.

The paper, which first appeared in **THE JOURNAL OF POPULAR CULTURE** has been reprinted in the Vol. 2, 1980, number of **THE JOURNAL OF UFO STUDIES** (Center for UFO Studies, 1609 Sherman Ave., Suite 207, Evanston, IL, $7.50 per issue, $15 for semiannual sub.) The authors are able to sift many interesting statistics from the data, and aside from their excellent work, their survey is all the more valuable because of its uniqueness - we doubt if this field has ever been researched similarly by others.

Drs. Stupple/Dashti also give Saucerian Press readers a clean bill of health in another area: they are definitely are **NOT** cult oriented. They are not part of a larger occult social world, and are interested in occultism only when they are related to UFOs. Nor are they "joiners." Only 12 percent belong to 'occult and religious groups' that study UFOs, and only 10 per cent belong to such "scientific" groups.

"The Saucerian Press readership is a collectivity of people who share a common interesst in the folklore that has developed around flying saucers. The majority do not belong to groups that share this collective interest."

A study of the demographics convince the authors that ".... there is reason to believe that Saucerian Press readers are reasonably well integrated into society."

Thish contains 11 other papers by well known academicians and Ufologists, including J. Allen Hynek, David Swift, Richard Hall, and even Peter Kor whom we haven't heard from since the Ray Palmer **FLYING SAUCERS** magazine days.

Cops Chase Saucers

Readers intrigued by Maj. Colman VonKeviczky's address to the House of Lords UFO Study Committee will also wish to read another address to that body by AF Maj. Hans C. Peterson, Danish Royal Air Force Ret., complete text of which is reproduced in current **THE SBI REPORT** ($15 per 7-ish year, Scientific Bureau of Investigation, Inc., 23 MacArthur Ave., Staten Island, NY 10312). Editors and International Directors Peter Mazzola and James FIllow are police officers who do a fine job of tracking down and bringing in fascinating UFO articles and reports.

Dauntless Duo

Hard working Robert S. Easley and Rick R. Milberg perform an accomplishment almost unheard of in the saucer world and which is overshadowed only by the excellent material they publish: the Cleveland UFO veterans (1) consistently maintain frequency of 12 issues per year with their **NORTHERN OHIO UFO GROUP NEWSLETTER** ($10 per year which includes full membership, 3403 W. 119th St., Cleveland, OH 44111 216-826-0225). And, (2) seemingly not content with this work schedule, they also publish **THE HILBERG-EASLEY REPORT** (No price of frequency given), a newsy, informal Newsletter-style sine which includes .lotsa editorial comments and letters from readers. Issue No. 2 gives an informal history of the modern saucer era in an article, The Nostalgia of UFOlogy," by Easley, and reviews of movies, books and television on our favorite subject.

Also Notable and Recommended:

UFO NEWSCLIPPING SERVICE ($5 per monthly issue, Route 1, Box 220, Plumerville, AR 72127) saves its subscribers the enormous cost of maintaining a costly newsclipping service of their own. Publisher Lucius Parish foots the initial bill, then prints the best clippings by offset reproduction in facsimile form. The March, 1981, clippings comprise twenty large 8 1/2 x 14' pages. The relatively high annual freight is softened by a monthly payment system.

THE NEW ATLANTEAN JOURNAL (Bimonthly $7.00 per year, $1.50 per issue, 5963 32 Ave. No., St. Petersburg, FL 33710) serves up a varied dish of subjects such as UFOs, Lost Atlantis, Monsters and other anomalies, subterranean worlds and you name it in nice fat issues (Currentish contains 62 pages). Editors Joan and Patrick O'Connell have bought a Radio Shack computer to handle their growing mailing list, which we can also recommend, along with the zine, to list renters in the New Age field. Saucerian Press has rented the subscription list twice, with excellent results. The publication must also be paying off for its advertisers, considering the amount of space bought in the Spring, 1981, issue reviewed.

The Dero and Tero should beware of the growing success of **SHAVERTRON**, described as The

Only Source of Post-Deluge Shaverania," by editor Richard Toronto (Quarterly, $6.00 per year, 309 Coughlan St., Vallejo, CA 4590). "Shaveranie of course refers to the legendary Richard S. Shaver and his theories of underground cavern civilizations, but the zine also keeps up with the times. For instance, the Summer, 81, ish also reports on 'Strange 'Roads' in New Mars Pictures."

Finally, what reader would be completely informed without **THE HOLLOW HASSLE**, the quarterly publication of THERA (The Hollow Earth Research Association)! **HASSLE** covers such subjects as polar and cavern entrances and exploration, Inner Earth realms such as Shamballah and Agharta, Indian legends, book reviews, and letters ($6.00 per yr, PO Box 255, Sante Fe, NM 87501.

THE MYSTERY OF CORAL CASTLE

====================================

----By James W. Moseley--
(Special to The NEWSLETTER)

The rush of tourist traffic speeds along U.S. Highway No. 1, connecting Miami with Key West, and traversing one of the most scenic areas of our country. A few vacationers see the garish tourist signs and stop for an a few minutes, but the marvel they witness seems obscured by the bursting beauty of sunlit beaches and blue oceans along the coast of Southern Florida.

I also stopped, intentionally to scoff, but stayed for many hours to wonder! Then I returned, again and again, whenever I visited the area. I thought that one of the greatest mysteries since the construction of the Pyramids of Egypt could be solved by investigation and common sense. But I was wrong!

The haunting mystery of **CORAL CASTLE** may **NEVER BE EXPLAINED WITHIN OUR LIFETIMES!**

The main tower of Coral Castle. The secret of its construction died with its builder in 1951 (Photo by Fred Broman).

When Latvian immigrant Edward Leedskalnin arrived at its site, no stream of autos whizzed by. For that was during the early 1920s, when Highway One was only a trail, used mainly by native Indians and a few settlers. But in that lonely and desolate place began the lifetime project of the immigrant, which would culminate in a mystery never, even to this day of space travel, cracked by science!

He first built a house for himself with logs cut from surrounding pine trees. Next he began, single-handedly and working entirely alone, the construction of Coral Castle.

The Castle is set on a ten acre tract, and the Castle proper is surrounded by an eight foot wall made of huge blocks of coral rock, each weighing several tons. The tower, yhich occupies one corner of the Castle, and is shown in an accompanying illustration, contains more than 160 tons of coral rock. Each block making up this huge two story building weighs nine tons. The first floor was used as a workshop, and the second housed his living quarters. During his lifetime the eccentric builder would allow curious visitors to pass through the grounds of the Castle, and he even took pleasure in showing them around. But no one was ever allowed into the tower, and an air of mystery prevailed around those quarters, made even more dramatic by superstitious Indians who claimed they heard strange humming sounds from the premises and feared mysterious 'fire birds' which visited the area during the night.

Leedskalnin died in 1951 without a will or heirs, having never married, and without relatives in this country. His land and Castle thus passed to the State of Florida, which disposed of it at auction to a tourist attraction developer who opened it to the public soon thereafter. As a result, anybody traveling in that area can ponder the enigma first hand for a modest admission price.

To enter Coral Castle the tourist first passes through a "swinging gate,' a triangular block of stone weighing three tons which turns with only a slight push. In the center of the rear wall there is a much larger such stone gate weighing nine tons, but so perfectly pivoted and balanced that a child can turn it!

Perhaps his greatest achievement, however, was not the unbelievable feats of moving and raising the immense coral quarried elements, but **HIS SUNDIAL**! I have never seen or heard of another like it anywhere in the world. Without more than a secondary school education in his native Latvia, he was able to build the ingenious device which, when properly understood, gives the time correctly to within two minutes **ALL YEAR AROUND**!

But still of primary interest is the question of **HOW** Leedskalnin, a man weighing little more than a hundred pounds, was able to move these huge coral rocks, weighing as much as 35 tons, without help from anyone. When queried about this he would explain crypticaly that he had rediscovered the method used in the construction of the Pyramids, then say no more.

Despite the tremendous engineering feats displayed in his work, only simple hand tools were found in the Castle after his death!

True, when he died, the Castle was looted, and some key pieces of machinery and other evidence may have been stolen. Throughout his life-time he had refused to demonstrate any of his techniques, though he did admit, on several occasions, that he

believed that other planets were inhabited. But he made no claims that they might be visiting the Earth, or had possibly assisted him in his construction work!

Scientists studying the Castle at first hoped the little educational booklets privately printed by the builder would provide clues to his techniques. But they were disappointed.: Although the publications dealt with magnetism (which the author considered to be the "key to the universe"), they outlined very simple experiments, involving mundane devices such as automobile batteries, ordinary magnets, used car parts, and other common items which he obtained by rummaging through junk yards. If Coral Castle had been built by the implementation of some secret discovery involving electromagnetism, there was no hint of it in anything he published.

My own conclusion indicates that Leedskalin **MUST HAVE HAD SOME SORT OF OUTSIDE HELP**, though one cannot envisage who or what that might have been! I am most skeptical (and have said so in print) of the claims of Von Daniken and his "ancient astronauts,' stories but such an explanation may be the only present one to make any 'sense,' -until, hopefully, some scientist may find a more logical solution!

In the daytime, when hurried tourists, with their bawling children impatient to go on to Disney World, crowd the Castle grounds, it is easy tc be skeptical. But when night falls, and the crowds thin out, and you can wander around the complex alone - well that is a different story. As the "cross-hairs" of the giant stone obelisk in the rear of the Castle (made of two wires like a gun-sight) line up perfectly with the North Star, it is then that you feel an otherworldly presence, start humming the '2001' movie theme and get a mist in your eyes.

FROM:
SAUCERIAN PRESS, INC.
BOX 2228
CLARKSBURG, WV 26301

BULK RATE
U.S. POSTAGE
PAID
JANE LEW, W.V.
Permit No. 2

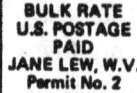

www.ingramcontent.com/pod-product-compliance
Lightning Source LLC
Chambersburg PA
CBHW080734020726

47503CB00010B/2912